Outcast County

It all started with the discovery of three dead men, each of whom had been shot from ambush. Blake Durant did the decent thing and buried them, and that should have been the end of it. But then he met up with Ben Adamson, discovered that the men had been working for him, and decided to help the old-timer drive his cattle into the next town down the trail.

That was when all hell broke loose. There was an attempt to steal the cattle, and in the process Durant was accused of a cold-blooded killing and sentenced to hang.

Loyal to the end, Ben Anderson fought tooth and nail to save him from the trumped-up charge … but that only led to even more problems, including a terrifying manhunt and, finally, an audacious plan to get even with the bad men who ruled Outcast County.

Outcast County

Sheldon B. Cole

A Black Horse Western

ROBERT HALE

First published by Cleveland Publishing Co. Pty Ltd,
New South Wales, Australia
First published in 1967
© 2020 Mike Stotter and David Whitehead

This edition © The Crowood Press, 2020

ISBN 978-0-7198-3131-7

The Crowood Press
The Stable Block
Crowood Lane
Ramsbury
Marlborough
Wiltshire SN8 2HR

www.bhwesterns.com

Robert Hale is an imprint
of The Crowood Press

ONE

DOOM TRAIL

Two of the dead belonged to Carver City. No one knew where they had come from. The streets were dark when they rode in and converged on the Lucky Lady Saloon and took their places along the counter; grim-faced men with bitterness etched into their trail-grimy features. They drank their drinks, ignored the townsmen and didn't even bother to talk to each other.

Sheriff Luke Appleby had been informed of their presence but he was late going down to check on them. Before he arrived, another stranger, Blake Durant, had entered the saloon. As Hap Dooley, the barkeep, told it later to Appleby, Durant had come casually through the batwings. A man, later identified as Sonny Balsam, had drawn his gun.

The first shot went an inch wide of Durant and tore a splinter from a still-swinging batwing. Then the fight was on.

Dooley said he saw all of it, and he told about it in full detail, although some skeptics wondered later how he could have seen anything from the floor behind the counter. Durant, said Dooley, threw himself to the floor. His gun had come out of his holster even before his shoulder hit the boards. Durant's first bullet killed Balsam, and his second tore the throat out of Sed Danielson. His third shot missed Muller, but then his fourth caught him in the chest, killing him instantly. The other two lit out through the back door. The echo of their horses' hoof beats had barely died when Sheriff Appleby arrived and learned that three men were dead.

Appleby's decision was the only one open to him. He told Blake Durant to leave town. There was nothing to hold him for, but the town didn't want Durant's kind cluttering up their streets. The only thing Blake Durant got from Carver City was a parting wave from Little Pino, only survivor of the Pino family from San Maradas. On his ride out of town on his blue-black stallion, Sundown, Blake Durant worried about Little Pino's future. Orphaned at thirteen, his swarthy skin an invitation for scum to badger him, Pino would need a lot of friends if he was to live to be big enough to fight his own battles.

Little Pino had only one friend, and tears flowed from his sad, questioning eyes when he saw Blake Durant ride away.

Carver City had nothing but terrible memories for him; a sister raped and killed, a father butchered going to her assistance, an older brother shot down before he could get to his gun. If it had not been for Blake Durant, the stranger who had happened by and read the sign correctly, Little Pino would have no fond memories to sustain him.

So the Mexican boy rode his mule the other way out of Carver City, and went into a loneliness that Blake Durant knew only too well.

The sun was high. A blisteringly hot wind cut its way down the steep slopes. Even along the valley floor, there was no breath of coolness. Blake Durant veiled his eyes against the sun's glare and smelled death in the air. Sundown caught the scent too and his action was proppy as he responded to the prod of Durant's boots. Man and horse were the only moving things along the long, narrow valley.

When he reached the valley's end, Durant worked up the final slope patiently. The air was still filled with dust and there was no breeze to drift it along. Into the haze of heat and dust, Durant rode, remembering Carver City, the men he had killed, and the little Mexican left to fend for himself. He spared no thought for Balsam, Muller or Danielson. Boot Hill could have them with his compliments.

At the top of the slope, Sundown stopped dead. His head lifted and his nostrils flared. Then Durant saw the three bodies, piled together, a scattering of dead branches partly covering them. Durant backed Sundown away and came out of the saddle. He removed his golden bandanna and mopped his sweating brow. Standing there, he made an arresting figure against the heat-seared country, wide of shoulder, deep-chested and slim-waisted, a man taller than six feet. His range clothes and boots showed the wear of travel, weather and time. Only the bandanna was clean.

He finally walked to the pile of bodies and discovered dried drops of blood on the shoulder of a rock. Had a survivor, weakened from his wounds, done what little he could to cover his slain friends?

Blake Durant stopped wondering and took the small spade from his saddlebag. The bodies buried, he followed the tracks of a man through the trees until he saw where a horse had been tethered. Looking into the dust-choked distance beyond the swirling heat devils of the prairie he saw vague movement. But the longer he looked, the less he could make out of that shapeless blur.

Returning to Sundown, he climbed into the saddle and let the horse pick its way down to the second valley. Through the heat of noon he rode, letting the big black make its own pace. Afternoon came and went and finally some of the heat left the day under the wash of a breeze. By then Durant had reached the end of the valley, and before him stretched a wide, treeless plain. At its end he saw a herd of cattle. Tailing the herd was a single rider.

Durant touched Sundown into a canter and gradually pegged back the herd and its lone attendant. But when he was only a couple of hundred yards away, the rider suddenly bore off to the left, raced for a brush thicket and disappeared.

Durant slowed Sundown. If this was a survivor of the valley massacre, he wasn't surprised that the man was wary. He made for the thicket and pulled rein minutes later when he saw the horse standing unattended. Blake moved Sundown beside the other horse and carefully stepped through the brush. Then, as he stepped into a barren clearing, a shot blasted.

Before Durant could call out, a bullet holed his range coat and another belted the hat from his head. He went to the ground and rolled as more shots rang out. Then, for what seemed a long time he lay flat and listened. There was no sound from below him. He rose to a crouch and inched forward. Another shot sent a scatter of brush into his eyes. But he held his fire.

Then a haggard, red-eyed face appeared before him. Blake heard the bellow of a curse and saw the gleam of a lifted gun.

Blake Durant threw himself forward and sent a vicious right-handed punch. The man's gun exploded and the bullet went within an ace of holing Durant's head. But his fist had hit home and the man's legs buckled. However, the hate riding the man was backed by devils of fury and he swung the gun again blindly, lashing out like a maniac. Blake ducked under the handgun and cracked a short left onto the point of his stubbled jaw. The man went down on his back, gave a grunt and then his head rolled.

The bloodshot eyes opened. The man lay there with his head on a pile of brush. The old man looked to his right, then to his left. He lifted a hand and touched his bullet-smashed shoulder, then winced as pain lanced into him. After a moment his gaze settled on Blake Durant.

Durant held a steaming mug of coffee out to him. "Have this."

The old man hesitated before raising himself to a sitting position. He rubbed the point of his jaw as he looked over the prairie where the herd of cattle had stopped and bunched, their backs dulled by dust and shapeless in the twilight. Then he took the mug of coffee.

"Who are you, mister?"

"Name's Blake Durant. I came this way from Carver City, saw three dead men and buried them. Then I kept riding and saw you. You must have taken me for somebody else."

The old man nodded and sipped at his coffee. Color began to come back into his leathery cheeks. He leaned forward, disregarding the pain from his shoulder wound and hooked his arms about his knees. He breathed in deeply.

"Yeah, I took you for one of the bunch that jumped us early this morning. Those three you found were hired hands of mine, taken on in Sonora. Good men. They didn't have much of a chance but they made the most of what they had. That other bunch rode off with a few bullets in them, too."

Durant listened attentively while he looked down at the night-settled herd, then he said, "When you're ready, I'll take a look at that shoulder. Since you've carried it all day, it's likely giving you hell."

The old man nodded, transferred the mug to his left hand and pushed out his right. When Blake shook his hand he said, "Ben Adamson. I'd be obliged for any help you can give me. For those shots I fired at you, I can't say much more than …"

"Forget it," Blake said as he continued to check the country below them. He didn't mention it to Adamson, but he wondered why a bunch of hellions had made a raid, killed three men and then left a lone survivor to go on his way. Maybe they had been harder hit than Adamson thought. Durant moved about, getting the saddle cramp out of his legs. Even now there was a quality of indifference about him. He was a man who lived in continual expectancy of trouble, not looking for it but always prepared.

His coffee finished, Adamson sat hunched over. He shivered although sweat glistened on his brow and cheeks. Durant wet a piece of clean blanket with boiling water and walked across to him. He tilted Adamson's shoulder back and pulled the shirt free of Adamson's left shoulder. As he dabbed the blood away, he looked warily about him. Everything was quiet. It was a good quiet which the cattle themselves would disturb if there was danger close by. Durant found the wound to be deep and ugly. He fetched a bottle of whiskey from his saddlebag, and after saturating the wound with it, offered the bottle to Adamson. The rancher's eyes sparked but he shook his head.

"Go on," Blake prompted him, and this time the old rancher took the bottle and had a long drink.

He breathed in deeply and then Durant bandaged his shoulder. Moments later Adamson got to his feet and stood drawing air into his lungs and looked thoughtfully at the fire.

"They might come back, Durant. I don't see why they wouldn't. They've got me beat."

"Not yet," Durant said. "How far do you have to take the herd?"

"Eighty, ninety miles."

Eight days, maybe nine, Durant calculated. He kicked dirt over the fire, then pulled Sundown free of the brush and turned him about. Adamson studied Durant more intently, rubbing a hand across the bandaged shoulder. It felt a lot better, but he knew without asking Durant that a sawbones would be needed eventually.

When Blake swung up and held Sundown checked, waiting for him to mount, Adamson licked his dry lips and cleared his throat. "What about you, Durant?"

"I'll tag along."

The bloodshot eyes gleamed with relief and gratitude. "I can't pay much. I had that understanding with the other three I hired. They were going my way and didn't mind."

"I don't mind either," Durant told him.

For the first time Ben Adamson smiled then, but went to his horse and, hiding his face, swung into the saddle. Blake saw him draw in a quick, ragged breath but then he was smiling again.

"Meant to use the night as much as I could," Adamson said. "Had hoped to reach Outcast County tomorrow sometime. No more than fifteen miles up."

"No water for the cattle here anyway," Durant said.

"Creek another five miles on. We'll give them a few hours rest and then keep going, okay?"

Blake shrugged. "It's your herd. I'm just along for the ride."

"I hope that's all it will be for you," Adamson said and then he led the way down the slope. They got the cattle bunched and moving slowly in quick time. When the herd was pushing on across the wide, moonlit plain, Adamson came back to Durant who had been riding drag. His face looked a lot younger because the soft moonlight didn't show the scars of time. He sat straighter in the saddle, appearing to draw on reserves of energy.

For a mile they rode close, enjoying the cool breeze, watching the bobbing backs of the steers. Then Adamson said, "You ever met a man who never got a break, Durant, not once in his life?"

"I've come across unlucky people," Durant said.

"Well, you've just met another one. I'm not grumblin', mind you, or complainin'. Guess I've asked for all I've ever got, maybe even looked for it. But nothing ever seems to go right for me. From the very beginning, things have worked against me." Adamson frowned. "I worked damn hard as a boy, hard as any man could. I saved my money, too, didn't spend wildly like so many others did. I always had it in mind to have a place of my own one day, to lick wild country into shape, fence it, stock it, see things I'd planted grow." He wiped his brow with a finger and turned his head to look behind.

"Well, in time I got enough money together to buy a place. Not much in some folks' eyes, but it was mine and it had my brand on it. I bought some good stock and set down to work. First year was fair enough, in fact now I look back maybe it was the best year I ever had. In the second year the drought hit me and stayed with me for the third. I borrowed from the bank to keep going. Had a fair fourth year, paid back something and met my wife-to-be. Maybe I shouldn't have married her, although I don't regret a minute I had with her. She was a good woman, stout and made to last, and I didn't hear one word of complaint or criticism pass her lips in the fifteen years we struggled together. We held on, mainly because of our daughter."

Blake listened, wondering how many stories like this a man could hear if he stopped in the one place on the frontier long enough.

15

"Bess died of some ailment nobody could understand. I had her to three doctors in a year but none of them could help. She lost weight, got listless, finally couldn't hardly get about. They were the bad days, Durant, watching her shrivel up and die and not being able to do anything for her. When she went, I had the girl to look after, rear, teach things to." He sucked in breath and muttered something to himself. Then his gaze swung to Durant and there was a deep sadness in his eyes.

"I failed at that too. I was too busy, had too much to do. I couldn't do anything for Joyce. She needed a mother. She loved me, but I'm a man. She just kinda tolerated me. Then she needed other things, other people. She left and I couldn't do anything to stop her."

Blake Durant pulled his whiskey bottle out and sipped it. He wiped the neck and handed the bottle across to Adamson who hesitated before taking it. He drank sparingly and nodded his thanks.

"When Joyce left I kinda mooned about for a time, but then I pulled myself together. I figured life would just have to go on. I had a good season and my place finally turned green on me, grassed so good I just couldn't let it waste away. I borrowed enough money to buy this herd and had some kind of future looking at me. I figured that maybe one day I could show Joyce a place where she wouldn't mind living. Then this last damn trouble hit me."

Adamson mopped his brow and worked his fingers about the grubby collar of his old shirt. "Three good men dead. If they hadn't teamed up with me, they'd be alive now."

"You can't blame yourself for that," Blake said.

Adamson's eyes grew angry. "Who the damn hell else can I blame, Durant? I'm bad business. I've always been bad business. I've tried harder than most men but there's a curse on me. Maybe that curse'll rub off on you. Maybe you should move along and mind your own business instead of tackin' onto a damn old jinx."

Blake gave a slow smile. "Maybe you should save your energy for the ride tomorrow, Adamson. That kind of talk just doesn't fit my picture of you."

Adamson's stare was hard for a moment, then he matched Durant's grin. "Yeah, maybe I should just shut up and count my blessings, Durant. I'll check the trail ahead. We must be getting close to that water and I don't want to let the steers stampede for it."

Adamson rode on and Durant drew memories from his mind and dwelt on them ... Louise Yerby standing on her father's porch, just looking at him, her eyes smiling ... Louise, saying nothing because she didn't need words to communicate ... Louise, who had meant everything to him, gone. Durant pulled at his gold bandanna, a gift from Louise, then he closed his eyes. So many long trails behind him. So much searching.

He forced himself back to the present. Adamson needed him. Blake Durant would stay with this old frontiersman until he was safely home. Between them was a bond of loneliness. Every trail he took seemed to bring him to undeserved misery and hardship. He had taught himself to act on instinct alone. He did things that had to be done and he would keep doing so until Louise released him.

He was pushing his horse down the side of the herd to steer back a couple of strays when he heard Adamson call, "Water ahead."

Blake gave him a wave and drew back to the rear of the herd. The cattle moved faster, then began to run. Blake let them go. He watched as they reached the narrow creek and settled down to drink, then he rode Sundown into a clump of trees.

TWO

NOTHING FOR PIONEERS

Outcast County loomed up before the herd, a sprawling town of houses, stores, barns and shacks set out in helter-skelter fashion. The streets seemed to have been laid as an afterthought. The main street was a long, winding thoroughfare that opened up broadly and cornered five times before it petered out at the prairie's beginning. Riding back to Durant, Ben Adamson, still looking tired, shouted:

"Don't know much about the place except that years ago they had town corrals when the railroad used to come through. I reckon we should corral them and see what happens from there."

"Sounds the logical thing to do," Blake told him.

They had worked the right side of the herd into a swing when gunshots sounded. Adamson looked worried but Blake went about his work effectively, pushing the cattle along the back of the town until they reached the yards. A tall, lean, clean-shaven man in businessman's clothes dropped off the porch of an office building. Then, skirting the yard, he hurried to open the gate Ben Adamson was approaching at the head of his herd. Adamson, finally seeing the townsman, drew rein, and after giving him a wave of recognition cut back along the side of the slow-moving herd to assist Durant. It took them only five minutes or so to get the herd into the yards. The lean man closed the gate and sat on its top rail, long legs dangling, a spent cigarette drooping from his lips. His eyes were dark and deep-set, revealing nothing.

"Ben Adamson, from Bible Creek way, mister. These your yards?"

"Yep, all mine. Glad to have them filled. Name's Weedon, Reg Weedon."

"May be only for a night, Weedon," Adamson said. "I struck some trouble coming up the plains and I'll have to sign on another couple of hands to help me get these steers home. You can maybe help me in that."

"Sure, sure," Weedon said affably. "Plenty of spare hands in town looking for work. Pity about you only stayin' one night, though, but I guess a man has to be thankful for small blessings."

"I'll pay a fair price, Weedon," Adamson said, then he waved towards Durant. "Friend of mine, Blake Durant. He's the only man besides myself with the right to check out them steers."

Weedon nodded, his dark eyes clouding just a little. Blake had no idea why. Weedon dropped his boots to the ground and looked the cattle.

"Nice, healthy looking bunch, Adamson. What was the trouble you mentioned?"

"Three men killed," Adamson said, his voice high and angry. He touched his shoulder. "Got to see the sawbones myself and then make a report about it to the sheriff. Where do I find those gentlemen?"

Blake saw a gleam of amusement in Weedon's eyes then. Weedon said, "Doc's place is right across the street and the jailhouse is seven doors up. Traversi, he's the sheriff, will be right interested to hear your story, Adamson."

"And I'll be right keen to fill him in on the details," Ben Adamson tossed back. "You going to stay and watch these beeves for me while I do that other business?"

"Goes with the price," muttered Weedon. He stole a careful look Blake Durant's way and Blake had the feeling that he was being measured. He ignored the man. The cattle had settled down peacefully as

21

he turned his horse away. He and Adamson crossed the street together, then Adamson said,

"You go on, Durant. I'll catch up with you in the saloon after I've talked to the sheriff and we'll have some drinks and some grub."

"Fine," Blake told him and went on. He rode the crooked, dusty main street, taking in the towns-people he passed. To him they looked an ordinary bunch, but a couple of cowhands, one wearing a double gunbelt, eyed him speculatively. Blake reined in outside the wide-fronted garishly painted saloon and thought briefly of Carver City and another saloon which had held a lot of big trouble for him.

He came out of the saddle. This was not Carver City. This was Outcast County, and although the town didn't impress him much, he had no reason to expect it to be as trouble-riddled as Carver City had been. Sundown was drinking from the trough when Blake pushed open the swing doors. A bellow of noise hit him in the face and he stopped momentarily, looking around. The place was crowded. Men were packed along the walls behind the card tables and a tight bunch were at the bar counter. The barkeep, a ruddy faced individual in a rye-stained apron and unruly red hair hanging across his tired eyes, was sweating at serving the customers on his own.

Durant made his way through the noisy crowd until he reached an end of the counter. He dropped some loose change on the boards and waited. When the sweating barkeep came, he ordered a double whiskey. He had so much dust in his throat, the drink had no taste as it went down. He ordered another and took his time with it.

He'd turned his back to the counter and was looking at the customers closest to him when a big, rough-faced cowhand jumped to the top of the piano in the far corner of the room. He was wide-shouldered and deep-chested and as burly in the waist as a bear. Thick, heavily muscled arms waved as his voice boomed out, demanding silence.

The silence was a long time in coming and in fact the big man had to bellow angrily before most of the noise died. Above the remaining commotion, he shouted:

"Listen here now, damn you! Everybody quiet. There's gonna be some fun here if you want it."

Blake Durant watched the big man look in every direction as his boots scraped the varnish off the piano top. The pin-headed piano player below him, looking up anxiously, had his mouth open in protest but no words of censure came from him.

The noise faded and some of the customers began to bunch up near the piano.

The big man's rugged face broke into a smile. "That's better now. Knew you folks wouldn't mind quietenin' when a man has somethin' important to say." He lifted his glass and gulped off the rest of a beer, then he tossed the empty glass down to the red-faced piano player. He wiped his mouth on his sleeve and grinned wider. Then he beckoned to someone in the crowd. "Come on up now, Bede, and show yourself to those who don't know you."

There was a shuffle of movement in the crowd packed around the piano and then another big man planted his boots on the piano keys. The discordant sound brought howls of appreciation.

Somebody called, "Don't you know another tune, Strawbridge? Heard that one too damn many times."

There was loud laughter. Strawbridge waved his hands for silence again, then he grabbed the second big man by the shoulder and planted him at his side.

"This here's my brother, Bede. My name, for those of you who ain't had the pleasure of knowin' me, is Bo. Bede and me, we come outa the same egg thirty years ago and we kinda grew the same. But neither of us has growed so powerful that we can scare too many people in a wild-livin' bunch like we got here today."

24

"Was that a lizard's egg, Strawbridge, or maybe a coon's?" came a voice from the side. Bo Strawbridge glared down, trying to pick out the jester from the sea of rough faces. When nobody ventured to pick out the speaker, he made a gesture of dismissal and went on:

"That joker now, he ain't exactly the kind I'm talkin' to so he better shut down till I'm through." Bo Strawbridge punched his brother Bede in the chest and said, "Bede and me will lick any two men in the saloon for two dollars. Cash up and winner take all."

There was a rumble of comment but no takers stepped out. Bo Strawbridge eyed his brother intently a moment and Bede gave him a nod.

"Okay then, gents, Bede and me'll take any three, same stakes."

There were still no takers and the talk died. Blake Durant let his gaze sweep the crowd. There were enough big men there to match the Strawbridge brothers, but the reluctance of them to come to grips with the twins suggested to him that the Strawbridges were as rough as they looked.

The silence was beginning to deepen when Blake saw a good looking dude stand up at the card table to the right of the piano player. Bo's look went speculatively to him and a glint of amusement entered his blue eyes.

"Cherry, are you takin' us on? Who you got backin' you? Couple of them gamblin' boys maybe want to try their luck?"

Cherry waved the challenge away and smiled broadly. "Nope, Strawbridge, brawling is not in my line, as you very well know." He held up a ten dollar bill and turned, showing it to the crowd. "The cards have been going my way tonight but I'm not a man to keep the good things of life to myself. Nor am I a man who will stand in the way of other men's enjoyment. So I'm offering this to the Strawbridge twins to put on a little fistic exhibition for us and belt themselves into silence so we can all have a little peace here."

Bo Strawbridge glowered down on him, but his eyes strayed finally to the ten dollar bill. He licked his lips and wiped his mouth on his sleeve. His brother Bede didn't respond in any way to Cherry's offer except to glance at Bo.

"If my offer is accepted as I think it will be," Cherry announced, "the ten dollars will be divided between these two equally, the loser to pay his share to the winner."

A roar of approval greeted this. Cherry lifted the bill above his head, tore it in half and handed the Strawbridge brothers the two halves.

"Bede," he said, "has beaten you twice before, Bo, as I remember it. So here's your chance to get something back on him and earn yourself some real fine drinking money at the same time."

Bede looked flatly at him as he took the half bill. "I'm Bede, Cherry. He's Bo."

"My mistake," Cherry said and pointed to Bede's bandanna. "And a natural one, as everybody will agree. So to make things simple for the men here, take that off."

As Bede's hand rose to his grimy bull neck, Cherry, eyes glinting with amusement, turned back to the crowd. "Bo will wear his bandanna and Bede won't. That way you men will know who you're backing. I'm laying them both. Take your pick, your six to my five for a start."

Bo Strawbridge glared down furiously at Cherry's sleek haired head and pinched his mouth between thumb and forefinger. But before he could make up his mind about the matter, hands reached to help him down. The crowd surged forward, some now assisting Bede down from the piano. In the onrush of bodies the piano player scurried away to the corner, looking tremendously relieved not to have been trampled underfoot.

Cherry cleared the card table and began to lay bets. By the time Bo Strawbridge had been carried outside, Cherry had filled the first page of a notebook. Blake Durant finished his drink and paid for another, telling the barkeep to take a drink to the piano player. He moved along to the back of the crowd and looked across a sea of heads into the yard. Bo Strawbridge had been lowered to the ground and Bede was standing near the fence, looking at the torn bill in his big left hand.

"I backed you, Bo," a tall cowhand told Bo Strawbridge, "and by hell you owe it to me to win for that dollar you borrowed a week back and ain't paid up yet. Win and we're square."

Bo studied the cowhand sourly for a moment before somebody pushed him towards his brother. Bede, mistaking this approach for enthusiasm on Bo's part, tossed his bandanna away, stuffed his half note into his pocket and slammed a fist into his brother's mouth. Bo staggered two paces and let out a roar.

"By hell, Bede, that weren't fair, not by any fig-urin', so I'll even that and then we'll see from there."

Bo stepped in and was hit again on the side of the head. His knees buckled and his face distorted with anger. He swung and hit Bede flush on the jaw and sent him reeling into the fence, then he closed in and hit Bede on the other side of the jaw. Bede rolled with the punch and the matter-of-fact interest he had shown in this fight now became raging fury. He charged at Bo, fists flailing mightily.

Blake Durant watched while Cherry moved about, calling changes of odds as the fortunes of the fight fluctuated. When Bo went down he called out two-to-one against Bo Strawbridge and a rush of men carried him back to the wall of the saloon. The crowd was yelling lustily now, encouraging the twin contestants. Bo, cursing and bleeding from a gashed mouth, heard the odds called against him and went wild.

There was a brutal savagery in the fight from that moment—toe to toe slugging with neither man giving an inch. For five minutes the twins, all kinship forgotten now, belted each other back and forth, from the fence to the saloon wall and across the yard, forcing the crowd to break continually to give them room. Cherry kept laying the odds until he had filled three pages of his notebook. He then closed the book, stuffed it in his vest pocket and found a position for himself on the back step. Blake Durant regarded him coolly, feeling that all this was unnecessary. He was sorry to see the big men so harshly exploited. Bo had just knocked the feet from under his brother when Blake Durant turned away. He found the barkeep standing behind him, craning his neck above Durant's shoulder to get a better view.

Blake said, "I'd like a drink."

The barkeep's mouth opened and his face clouded. "Hell," he moaned, "there's always some-body to spoil a man's fun."

"Never mind," Blake told him. "I'll help myself."

He eased the barkeep aside, ignored the dis-trusting look thrown at him, and crossed to the counter. When he'd had his drink, he turned to look at the backs of the crowd. Cherry was gazing intently at him, his face tight with interest. For a brief moment their eyes met. Then a roar from the crowd took Cherry's attention back to the fight.

The thud of punches continued until suddenly there was a gasp, followed by silence, that ended in the scrape of boots from the yard and then the stamp of boots on the saloon boards. Cherry crossed to the card table, laid out his money and began tidying it. A group of men, grinning, went over to him, hands held out for payment. The drinkers came in, talking excitedly. Durant learned that Bo had sent Bede crashing through the fence, then, heeling about in triumph, he'd pitched for-ward on his face, out cold.

Ben Adamson appeared at Blake's shoulder and pushed forward money for drinks. He looked any-thing but pleased with himself, and he explained gruffly, "The doc fixed me fine and says I'll be sore for a couple of weeks, but there's nothing to worry about. But that damned Traversi listened to my story of the raid and the killings like I was talking about the weather."

Blake asked, "No investigation?"

"Nope. He said it happened outside his town. Damn him, he's about the coldest-hearted damn …"

"Don't let it bother you," Blake tried to console him. "You've still got other worries."

Adamson nodded grimly and wiped sweat from his face. He had three quick drinks before he took time to check out the men about him. Most of the talk was still about the Strawbridge brothers' fight and Blake filled him in on the details. Adamson proved Blake's opinion of him to be correct when he muttered:

"That's a hell of a thing, lettin' kin beat the stuffin' out of each other."

Durant merely nodded. When Adamson had satisfied his thirst, Durant suggested a meal. They left the saloon and sought out the eatery, leaving behind them a saloon full of men drunk on whiskey and excitement.

Sheriff Red Traversi eyed his deputy, Lem Edey, calmly as the tall, boyish-faced lawman entered the jailhouse. Edey swiped the hat from his head, and ran his fingers through his thick, dark hair, grinning widely.

"What was the commotion about?" Red Traversi asked him.

"The Strawbridge pair again. Cherry wrangled up a fight between them and they beat themselves senseless. They're both still out in the saloon yard. I left them there."

Traversi stood up behind the desk and rolled his wide shoulders. He was forty years of age and looked younger. This he attributed to his ability to keep all his thought and movements down to the barest minimum. He refused to let anything cause him deep concern. At the same time he claimed he was capable of handling any situation, and this was his constant boast to the hero-worshipping Edey.

When Traversi walked around his desk, Edey tossed his hat idly onto it.

"The Adamson girl wants to see you," Edey said casually.

The words brought Traversi heeling about. Edey beamed at the surprise in the sheriff's face, then nodded his head.

"Yeah, she wants to see you. In her room. Guess maybe she's taken better stock of you than you figured, Red. If you don't want to go, I don't mind filling in for you."

Red Traversi's eyebrows arched. "Well, well," he said. "Been a while coming, ain't it?"

"You always were a waiter, Red. Guess maybe that's something else I can learn from you."

Traversi picked up his hat and fitted it to his head. He inspected himself in the tiny wall mirror and his smile broadened as he decided he was not the ugliest man in the world.

Walking to the door, he said, "Don't do anything about the cattle. Not yet. See Moulson and Day and tell them to lay low, just in case. If Weedon calls, tell him the same. We got all night and I don't see no reason to lock horns with Adamson's trail friend, Durant, unless it's necessary."

Edey nodded and Red Traversi went out. He strode along the boardwalk, taking in the cool evening air. Life was one big laugh for him and Maria was on hand when he needed her. Now the Adamson woman had thrown out a bait for him. He had no idea what she had on her mind. Even if it wasn't romance, he'd let Edey think he'd added another woman to his collection.

Traversi entered the saloon, spoke briefly to the barkeep, then checked the yard to find Bo and Bede Strawbridge sitting groggily against the broken fence. Traversi answered the greetings thrown his way and went up the stairs. He was unaware of the interest Dane Cherry showed in him as he climbed the stairs, but even if he had noticed it, Red Traversi was not a man to let that sort of thing worry him. He had a high respect for Cherry's ability with a gun, but this was his town and nobody could lock horns with him and expect to come out a winner.

He turned at the top of the stairway, removed his hat and smoothed down his thick red hair. Cleaning his palm on his shirt front, he knocked on a door marked with the numeral seven. The door opened in a moment and Traversi's gaze swept up and down the woman who stood there. He made no attempt to disguise his appreciation over what he saw.

The woman reddened and stepped back. "Come in, Sheriff Traversi. I'm grateful you could come."

"Pleasure is mine, Miss Adamson," Traversi said. After closing the door behind him, he took a keener look at her. She had delicate features and her eyes, dark and thoughtful mostly, were clouded now. She held herself with dignity and reserve and returned his look calmly.

"You've always been considerate to me, Sheriff Traversi."

"Ma'am, it'd be hard for any man to be otherwise."

Miss Adamson blushed a little more. But a smile touched her lips. Traversi crossed the room and stood against the wall looking back at her with the night noises drifting in from the street below the window.

"I ... I'd like to ask a favor of you," she said hesitantly.

Traversi regarded her calmly. "What is it?"

"It's about my father. I know you must have noticed the cattle that were brought to town just on sundown today, and the man who was with them."

"Two men," Traversi said.

"Yes. But I'm talking about the older one of them. He's my father, Ben Adamson. I haven't seen him for a year now, since I left home."

Traversi showed keener interest. "So?" he asked.

"I saw that he'd been hurt and he looked so tired. I think something troublesome has happened to him. When I left home we had a terrible argument and I'm not sure if he wants to speak to me again. But I am worried about him, driving all those cattle with only one man to help him, and wounded. We both know what a wild town this is, with so many men coming and going, and most of them not beyond causing a man with so many cattle some trouble. So ..." Her voice trailed off.

"So?" Traversi said.

Joyce Adamson passed the tip of her tongue across her lips and took in a slow, deep breath.

Her bosom rose and Traversi's eyes preyed on their roundness.

"I'd like you to help him if you could. He's old and stubborn but he's a good man. I'd be ever so grateful."

Traversi ran a big hand through his red hair, "How grateful, ma'am?"

Joyce stiffened. "Well, I'd be always in your debt, Sheriff Traversi. I don't know exactly how I could repay you. But I'd always think of you as a man kind enough to …"

"You could ask Cherry to do it for you," Traversi said, his voice thickening a little. "Why don't you do that?"

"But he's not the sheriff; you are. It's your duty to protect people."

"It was Cherry who helped you before, ma'am. What'd you give him for that?"

Traversi pushed himself away from the wall and took a step towards her. Joyce backed off in fright, letting out a tight gasp of alarm. She was immediately aware of his intentions and her face paled.

He said, "Dane Cherry, the dude man, with his fine manners and cool ways, he'd get plenty, wouldn't he, like he's been gettin' all along from you. Don't try to fool me, ma'am, I know what goes on in this town. You and him, you been havin' a real wild time together, ain't you?"

Joyce reached the wall and looked about anxiously.

But Traversi propped a hand up on the wall on one side and leaned towards her, blocking the way. He was grinning broadly now, clearly enjoying her uneasiness. His eyes went to her bosom and then down her stomach, hips and legs.

"No, you're wrong," Joyce cried out. "Dane Cherry is a friend of mine. He respects me."

"He's gettin' you, ma'am, and I been watchin' and knowin' for some time and been figurin' how to cut myself in for a slice of you. You got your hooks into me, ma'am, in a way that stops me sleepin' sound of a night." He shook his head and a curl of red hair fell across his right eyebrow. He didn't bother to put it back in place.

Joyce shook her head anxiously again. "But you have your own woman. You have Maria."

"Maria ain't you, ma'am. Maria is her and you are you and I aim to have some of you. All I want, in fact."

Joyce drove a hand at his chest but Traversi's hand clamped on her fingers, turning them back. Joyce let out a cry of pain and he brought her hard against him and held her there, her soft body flattened against his wide chest. He chuckled as she struggled and Joyce finally realized that he was enjoying the contact of her body. She tried to wrest her hand free to claw at him, but when his strength proved too much for her, she snapped:

"You wouldn't try this if Dane Cherry was here, would you? He'd fix you properly."

Traversi's smile faded and a hint of anger came into his eyes. "That dude couldn't do nothin' to me, ever, ma'am. Ain't nobody in this town could, so you just stop fightin' me and give me what I come for and maybe I'll see that your father ain't harmed."

Traversi tilted her head back and planted his lips on hers. When Joyce twisted away, he ran his mouth down the side of her neck, finally biting the top button off her blouse. He spat it onto the floor and pushed his face down into the swell of white flesh. Joyce cried out and fought him off fiercely, then the door opened and Dane Cherry burst into the room. Before Traversi could wheel about, Cherry's gun butt cracked down on the back of his head. Traversi's legs buckled under him, and his head hit his knees. He fell forward.

Joyce stepped back from him, face dead white.

"It's all right now," Cherry said.

Joyce lifted her hands to her face. She stood there, sobbing, while Cherry looked coolly at Red Traversi.

Finally he said, "Throw some things into a bag and let's get to hell out of this place."

Joyce quickly gathered some clothes from her dresser and packed them into a carpetbag. When Cherry escorted her out of the saloon the back way, she said:

"My father came with a herd of cattle this afternoon. I want to go to him."

Dane Cherry looked at her. "Your pa? That was him?"

Joyce nodded. "I've got to see him. Please, Dane."

Cherry shrugged. "Why not? Guess you'll be safe enough with him." He took her across the yard.

THREE

"YOU'RE GONNA HANG!"

The night wind was cool as Ben Adamson and Blake Durant moved along the corral rails, inspecting the cattle. The steers had settled down and were standing close-bunched, their heads down.

"First thing in the morning, I'll seek a couple of reliable hands," Ben Adamson told Durant. "I'd sure like you to tag along until I get the herd home. Then maybe you'll stay on a while. Be good to have somebody about the place for a change."

Blake nodded. Over a good meal of steak with lashings of thick rich gravy he had learned a lot more about Adamson. And what he learned he liked. Adamson was old stock, the kind that took

40

every hardship in his stride. He could see no barrier to their becoming firm friends.

Looking for Weedon, they continued on to the porch of the yard office. Adamson was climbing the narrow steps when a shot broke the silence. The echo of the shot had not died when a second bullet tore Blake Durant's hat from his head and a third smashed out the window of the office. Heeling about, his gun coming to hand speedily, Durant saw three furtive figures moving against the line of rails. The cattle were moving, shuffling about, lifting dust from the floor of the yard. Sparing a quick look Adamson's way, Blake saw that the old man had hit the porch boards.

He called out, "Stay put!" as he broke into a run. A volley of shots smashed into the porch rail, sending splinters flying. More shots cracked into the wall and bullets howled about Durant's head as he charged down to the end of the rails. The three gun hands had backed off a few yards and spaced themselves. Durant dropped to the ground and opened fire. He heard a man bellow in pain. A second emptied his gun and then broke into a frenzied run, leaving his two companions to fend for themselves.

With Durant's bullets smashing into the rails, the cattle began to mill about in panic. A section of the herd pounded the rails, threatening to break through and stampede into the prairie beyond the town. Durant realized that at any moment they would crash out, so he rose from the ground and ran across the open stretch, drawing the bullets of the attackers after him. Ben Adamson was shouting something at him when a bullet ripped through his flying range coat. He turned and saw a crouched figure outlined against the faint light from the street lamps.

Durant had no option but to shoot to kill. His gun bucked and two bullets pounded into the gun hand. The man spun, then he fell.

Turning sharply back on his own tracks, Blake Durant saw that Ben Adamson's gun was forcing the other two back down the rails. Now they broke into a run. Durant held his fire. In the silence which settled now, he and Adamson came together and walked the rails, then:

"Hold it there!"

Blake Durant turned his back to the rails. Before him, walking fast, was a tall man with a tin star on his shirt, his face indistinct in the bad light, a gun gleaming in his hand. Ben Adamson said tightly, "Leave this to me, Durant. I can handle it."

The lawman's face became more distinct as he came up until, finally, Blake could see his features clearly, bitterness dragging on his cheeks, set jaw and hard, black eyes.

As he stopped before Durant, the gun leveled, two other figures loomed up behind him.

The lawman growled, "Check him out," indicating with an abrupt wave of his hand the man lying unmoving on the ground. One of the other two went off and from a distance called back, "It's Rick Eggert, Lem. He's dead."

Blake saw the lawman's face jolt. His lips turned back in a snarl.

"You'll hang for this mister."

Ben Adamson stepped forward, saying, "Now hold on, Deputy. Best you get the facts straight."

"Shut down. I'm doing the talking here, mister."

"To hell I will shut down! These jaspers …"

The deputy stepped forward and palmed Ben Adamson back to the rails. Then he took Durant by the shoulder and shoved him forward. "Move!"

Blake went a step forward, then Ben Adamson lunged from the rails and grabbed at the deputy, who hurled him away again, as the other two closed in, guns ready. Adamson stopped dead under the threat of the guns and Blake Durant planted his feet wide.

"You'll hear me out," he said defiantly.

"Later, mister. I said to move, so do it. You killed the judge's son and Judge Eggert loved that boy. You're in a whole mess of trouble."

Blake drew in a ragged breath as Ben Adamson bought in again. "What kind of lawman are you, not letting an honest man speak his piece? I'm telling you, deputy, Durant here …"

"Shut him up," the deputy said coldly and one of the other two stepped forward and brought his gun butt down hard on Adamson's head. As the rancher fell, Deputy Lem Edey pushed Durant forward again and snarled out, "Leave him there. He won't be any trouble. Go get Red. And you, Day, fetch the judge."

Blake went stumbling after another shove from Edey. The deputy's gun dug into his back and he realized argument was useless here. They passed the dead man and Edey growled, "Mister, you done it now, real good."

Blake gave the dead man a look and then took in silence the deputy's constant pushing. They went across the street with the other two running off down the town. Outside the jailhouse, Deputy Edey drove his gun into Blake's back again and prodded him inside. The light of the big front room made Blake blink and before his eyes had become accustomed to the glare properly, Edey had his cell keys. He motioned for Blake to go ahead, then he held his gun on him in his left hand while he opened the cell door. When Blake hesitated, Edey grabbed his shoulder and hurled him inside.

Blake stopped just short of the low bunk and turned back to see the cell door shut on him. He turned fiercely to Edey, who answered his angry look with a sneer.

"The judge, he dearly loved his boy, Durant. Sit and think about that."

Blake made fists of his hands and tried to fight down his anger. The injustice of the affair rankled him. But for the moment he couldn't see what he could do to get himself a measure of justice. The cards were stacked against him.

Edey pounded back across the room and stood in the doorway, his body stiff with tension. A full minute went by before he called back, "They're comin' now, Durant, so if you know any prayers, start sayin' 'em."

Blake Durant walked to the cell bars and grabbed them hard. His mounting fury made his body go cold. He heard the footsteps coming fast up the board-walk and breathed a curse. Then he stood there and waited. There was nothing else he could do.

Joyce Adamson gave a gasp of horror as she saw her father being pushed along the street to the jailhouse.

"Hold it," Dane Cherry said and dropped a restraining hand on her arm. Joyce tried to pull clear but he tightened his grip, adding, "That looks like a mess of trouble. We'd better stay out of it for now."

"But that's Pa, Dane. What are they doing to him?"

"Looks like they're crowding him," Cherry said. "And they can sure do that real well. No sense in stepping into it, not after the trouble you've already had with Traversi. If they see us together, Traversi will come after my hide."

Joyce tried to twist away but she couldn't break Cherry's grip. They were in the shadows at the back of the yards where they had hurried when the shooting started. Knowing the threat of a cattle stampede, Dane Cherry had carefully picked his position against a store wall.

"They hit Pa, Dane. They knocked him down!"

"Seen that, but it's done now. Now listen to me, I can't get involved any more. You run into that and you can only make things worse. Besides, it looks like it's over."

Joyce Adamson bit her lip and pushed the hair back from her face. She watched anxiously as Deputy Lem Edey forced the big man across the street. When the other two went off, leaving her father lying on the ground, she sobbed.

"Please, Dane, let me go to him."

"Couple of more minutes and then we'll both go to him," Cherry said. He released his grip on her arm as Edey neared the jailhouse. When the other two had run down the main street boardwalk and Edey had taken his prisoner into the jailhouse, Cherry moved off. Joyce, keeping pace with him for a few steps, suddenly ran to where her father lay. By the time Cherry caught up with her, she had lifted her father's head from the dust. Tears ran down her cheeks.

Cherry said, "He'll be all right."

Joyce hugged Ben Adamson's head to her bosom. When the old man finally stirred, Cherry helped him to his feet. With Adamson slumped groggily against him, Cherry drew him back along the rails. Before they reached the end of the street, Adamson was struggling to fend for himself.

"Pa, are you all right?" Joyce asked.

Adamson opened his eyes, blinked and then looked at her disbelievingly. "Joyce?"

"Yes, Pa, it's me."

"How in all hell …" Adamson began, then he shrugged off Dane Cherry's grip and studied him frowningly.

Cherry explained, "You tangled with the town deputy, Adamson. They took your big friend off to the cells."

Adamson let out a curse. "They took Durant off?"

"At gunpoint. Seems he's got himself into a big parcel of trouble, which you better stay out of. Nobody can help him against that crowd."

47

Adamson eased Cherry aside. After giving his daughter a worried look, he snapped, "I've got to go to him. I have to explain how it was. Durant killed in self-defense."

"Killed who?" Cherry asked.

"The judge's son, they said. They wouldn't listen to Durant or me. I can't let them get away with this. I've got to back him up—I'm the only one who can."

Cherry smoothed down the ruffled front of his vest, feeling uncomfortably warm despite the coolness of the night wind. All his life women had meant trouble for him. Maybe Joyce Adamson was worth it, but he couldn't let himself get involved any deeper than he was. Of course, if Traversi knew who had hit him from behind, then it wouldn't matter.

"Look," Cherry said to Adamson, "I think you'd better keep well out of this. Eggert plays along with the sheriff and the deputy. The only help you can give Durant by putting your nose in further is to provide him with a cell mate."

Joyce saw indecision in her father's face and spoke. "Listen to Dane, Pa. He knows this town. And he's right. You can't beat them. Nobody can. The whole town bows to them."

"I don't give a damn about that!" Adamson snorted. "Durant's helped me getting my cattle this far and again just now." He studied them both, looking for understanding but seeing none in their faces. He then told them what had happened, beginning with the ambush on the trail drive and ending with the gunfight they had just witnessed.

"Can you expect me to leave a friend like that to fend for himself?" he asked finally, his voice hoarse with impatience.

Joyce, remembering the stubborn anger of her father in the past, knew that nothing she could say would deter him from his determination to stand by a loyal friend. So she remained silent, worried for him and for herself.

Dane Cherry answered curtly, "I'm telling you that any attempt to help Durant will only get you into deeper trouble, Adamson. There's a chance that Traversi and Edey won't be able to make their charge against Durant stick; a very slim chance. Until we know for sure, I suggest that you cool down." Cherry caught the concern in Joyce's face and sighed wearily. "But I've been a fool before," he muttered.

Joyce brightened immediately and touched his arm. "Then you'll help, Dane? What can you do?"

"I can drift across and see what's happening. Best you get your father to my place and lay low. And for hell's sake stay there till I come back. I'll report to you as soon as I know what's going on."

Joyce leaned forward and kissed him lightly on the cheek. "You're wonderful, Dane, just wonderful."

Ben Adamson studied Cherry more keenly now, noting his handsomeness, his good clothes and manners. He had never liked dudes, but in the present circumstances, hogtied as he was, he was prepared to accept the man's word.

"I'd be mightily obliged to you, Cherry," he said.

The gambler nodded. "I just hope this drifter, Durant, is worth it."

"You'll find he is."

Cherry flipped out his gun so effortlessly that Ben Adamson frowned. But then Joyce tucked her hand under his arm and stood on her toes to kiss him on the forehead.

"Oh, Pa, I've been such a fool!" she said. "Such a stubborn little hot-headed fool!"

Adamson put his arm about her slender shoulders and held her close. "We've both been just that girl," he said. "But I guess it will work itself out in time. What matters most now is helping my friend, Durant. Can you understand that?"

"Yes, Pa." She gave him a hug and smiled warmly at him; then, as she made to move off with him, their attention was attracted by noise further along the boardwalk.

Dane Cherry muttered, "Well, the hounds are out by the look of it. And in full force. Our esteemed sheriff, our respected Judge Eggert and their faithful hired hands. I'd best get moving." Cherry gave Joyce a nod and made his way along the yards. The cattle had settled down again. At the corner of the yards he stopped and watched two men lift the dead Rick Eggert from the ground and carry him into the jailhouse. Dane Cherry then walked slowly and thoughtfully across the street. He took up a position in the jailhouse laneway, produced a small cigar, bit off the end and lit it.

FOUR

THE LAW OF
OUTCAST COUNTY

Blake Durant watched the men file into the jail-house. The big man wearing a tin star he took to be Sheriff Red Traversi. To him, Traversi had all the marks of a hard case. He seemed cocksure of himself as he walked across the jailhouse floor and took hold of the cell bars.

"Murdered a man in my town, eh?"

"I killed in self-defense," Blake said.

Traversi snorted. "Ain't how I heard it, mister."

"Then you heard it wrong, Sheriff."

Red Traversi swept his hair back with a flour-ish and then, drawing his gun quickly, banged it against the bars. Durant pulled his hands away just in time to escape the gun and Traversi leered at him. Then, nodding his head, he stepped back. Deputy Lem Edey had directed two sullen-featured cowhands to seat themselves on a wall bench and now he turned and looked gravely at a thick-set, gray-haired man who stood framed in the jailhouse doorway.

Behind this frock-coated man's shoulders, two men stood facing each other and Blake Durant could see a dead man hanging limp between them.

Traversi turned, gave Durant his back and said tightly, "Bad night for you, Judge."

The other nodded and took two steps into the room. Looking straight at Durant, he muttered, "Bring my boy in. Lay him down careful."

The two cowhands entered with the dead man. They looked uneasily at Traversi who gave the room a sweeping look before he pointed to the end cell. "There," he said.

The cowhands went down the room and lowered the body to a bunk. One picked up a blanket from the top of a box, but before he could place the blanket over Rick Eggert's body, the judge said sternly:

"Don't cover my boy. I want to be able to see him."

Red Traversi watched the old man intently. When the judge came slowly across the room, taking his gun from his holster, the lawman frowned heavily.

"Listen to me," the judge said. "We have enough witnesses here to testify that this scum made a break for it while we were hearing his lies and got in the way of a bullet."

He lifted the gun and pointed it straight at Durant. Blake held his stare evenly and said calmly, "He came at me with a bucking gun, mister. It was him or me."

The judge's lips curled back derisively. "That your claim, mister?"

"It's the truth."

"It's a damned lie!"

The words slashed into the room's silence. Deputy Edey bit his lips and suddenly Red Traversi looked amused. But he gestured at the judge, saying:

"I've got a better way."

Judge Eggert jerked around. His gray cheeks were like pounded putty.

"A much better way," Traversi said. "Slower."

The judge's eyebrows climbed his heavily-lined forehead and disdain took hold of him.

"The noose," Traversi explained and ran a hand about his bull neck. "Slow and sure and a real spectacle. It'll serve notice on all jaspers who might be gettin' fool ideas that we run things right and ain't losin' our touch. Take a night to set the gallows up and we can use that time to spread the word. Come sunup, our killin' friend here will have done a heap of sweatin' and waitin'. Do him good."

Judge Eggert pulled on his gray cheeks and glared at Durant again. Lem Edey put in, "We ain't had a hangin' in months, Judge. Folks are likely to forget what one looks like."

Eggert glanced his way and took in a slow, deep breath. Seeing that he was still unconvinced, Red Traversi went on, "Got ourselves a courtroom, Joe, a presiding Judge and reliable witnesses. We enter it in the books so there ain't nobody can grumble about our law-enforcin'."

"Who cares about that, Red?" Eggert asked gruffly.

Grinning, Traversi thumped his chest. "Hell, I do, Judge. I got a reputation to think of."

Eggert was thoughtful for a moment and then he looked fiercely at Blake Durant. "The slow way is maybe the best. Deputy, take down the notes of the trial. Witnesses, come forward and say your piece."

The two men rose from the wall bench, exchanged satisfied looks and came across the room. Edey seated himself at the desk and began to write. Traversi lounged against the bars of the cell next to Durant's and made up a cigarette. His stare mocked Durant into muttering a curse.

"Day, testify on what happened," Eggert said.

The taller of the two cowhands straightened up and cleared his throat. Looking straight at Blake Durant, he said, "This here jasper walked up to Rick Eggert and shot him down cold. Wasn't no reason for him to do that because Rick never even had a gun."

Judge Eggert kept looking at Blake Durant. A nerve jumped in his temple and his lips were compressed and colorless.

"Peters?" he asked.

"Exactly the same, Judge. No mistake. There was plenty of light and we was right up close. Murder for sure."

"Any other witnesses?" Eggert asked.

There was no answer. Traversi lit his cigarette and blew out a mouthful of smoke. Eggert drew himself straight and gripped the bars of Durant's cell. His eyes narrowed and his lips curled back to reveal clenched teeth.

"Under the power invested in me by this community, and after hearing all evidence relating to the murder of Rick Alroe Eggert, I, Joseph Alroe Eggert, on this day of June, the …"

Eggert stopped short and eyed the deputy. "What's the damn date?"

"The tenth, Judge."

"… tenth, hereby sentence …"

Eggert's eyes blazed with renewed hatred as he looked at Blake Durant. "What's your damn name, mister?"

"Name's Durant, Blake Durant," Edey put back.

"… Blake Durant to be hanged by the neck till dead on the morning of the eleventh of June, at sunup. And may the devil take your soul!"

Traversi pushed himself from the wall and crossed to Judge Joe Eggert, sending an amused look Durant's way.

The name of the judge stuck in Durant's mind. He remembered back to Pinosa, a town on the fringe of the Platte River country … to a judge leaving a courtroom and taking on Billy Younger in the main street. Joe Eggert killed Billy Younger in a shoot-out when the evidence presented in court was insufficient to convict Younger of murder.

Blake looked at the old man more intently now. Five years. Joe Eggert had aged a lot in that time.

"Do all your court hearings stink, Eggert?" he asked.

Eggert shook the cell bars in his powerful grip. "Durant," he said viciously, "I'm gonna make the noose myself and put it around your stinkin' neck. Then I'm gonna release the trapdoor and watch you twist and squirm. My boy was all I had. I reared him to be …"

"You reared a dog, Eggert, in your own image," Blake Durant said.

Eggert shook the bars, his face growing purple. Traversi tried to pull him away, but Eggert smashed him back, shouting, "Damn you, mister, I'm gonna hang you personal! Then I'm gonna drag your body through the streets and lay it out for the buzzards and then I'll watch them tear you to pieces!"

Sweat ran freely down his face and his breath came faster and faster until he was choked up with fury. Traversi pulled him away and held him at a distance, saying, "Easy now, Judge. We done what we had to. No sense in letting it get away with you now. Durant'll hang and we'll drink to it tomorrow."

Eggert allowed himself to be eased across the room. He walked to the cell where his son lay uncovered and stared down at his death-gray face. The judge closed his eyes and mumbled to himself.

Traversi said lazily, "Lem, best get them nail hitters on the job right away. Work 'em through the night if needs be. You boys can go," he told the cowhands, Day and Peters. "And we're mightily obliged for your assistance." He frowned darkly. "But I ain't forgettin' you took on somethin' without consultin' me. Git now!"

Day and Peters moved quickly towards the front door. Edey lifted his arms above his head and worked his shoulders. Joe Eggert walked past

Durant's cell and went out without another word, his head bowed, his feet shuffling. As the door closed on him along with Day and Peters, Traversi blew smoke at the end of his cigarette and watched the sparks fly.

"Rick ain't no loss," he muttered. "Never was much damn good anyway."

Lem Edey grinned and went out to the board-walk. Looking at the long, winding main street of Outcast County he thought he was a very fortunate young man to have met so many important people so early in his life. He went off looking for the gallows builders.

Dane Cherry made his way into the back street and headed for home, a shack at the end of the main street.

Entering his yard, he found Ben Adamson and Joyce waiting under the overhang. He pulled out a fresh cigar, inspected it and lit it.

"Bad news," he said.

"What are they gonna do?" Adamson asked.

"Hang him."

Adamson's voice became a cry. "What?"

"They had a hearing. Judge Eggert presided, witnesses were called and notes taken. Durant was found guilty of murder and they're hanging him at sunup."

Joyce pulled back from her father, frightened by the fury bursting from him. Adamson paid her no heed now. "That's crazy, Cherry! Durant never murdered anybody."

Cherry drew on his cigar and shrugged. "I'm just telling you about the court finding, Adamson. You asked me to go and find out and I've done that. In the meantime I hope Joyce has explained the trouble we had with Traversi ourselves earlier tonight. She might also have told you that we've got a deep feeling for each other."

"To hell with that!" Adamson barked. "I'm only worried about Durant and getting him out of that darned jailhouse."

"That'll take some doing," Cherry told him.

"I don't care what it takes. I'm not standing by and see an innocent man hanged—and a damned good friend at that." Adamson plucked out his gun and inspected it. Joyce moved back to him, grabbing at his wrist. But he pushed her roughly away.

"Pa, what are you going to do?" she said. "You can't fight them. There're too many of them and they're mean and vicious. You'll get yourself killed."

Adamson snorted disdainfully at that. "No matter. Do you expect me to ride off and leave him there? Do you reckon I could stand living any place knowin' I backed off on him? I'll get him out, you'll see, and I'll give those scum something to think about for a while. Then I'll get my cattle and get to blazes out of this town."

Adamson moved quickly out of the shadows and looked towards the lights of the town. There was very little noise now and only a few people were moving about. He stopped, making his decision, and looked back at her, ignoring Cherry.

"If somethin' happens to me, girl, I guess you're old enough to look after yourself. Maybe it's Cherry you want. Well, I got no argument against that, though I'd like to know somethin' more about him before I give my consent. No matter about that either. If I pull this off, I won't have time to come back for you. It'd be too risky havin' you along anyway. You know where my place is, you're welcome to come back any time."

"Wait," Dane Cherry said. "That attack was an attempt to get your cattle, Adamson, or at least it was meant to get you and Durant out of the way. The next attempt won't fail, believe me. Those cattle have reached the end of their walk in this territory. Come a day or so, they'll get freighted out and Traversi, Eggert, Weedon and the deputy, Edey, will cut up the profits."

Adamson gaped at him. "You're loco, mister. What the hell damn foolery is that? Are you askin' me to believe that in a town this size, with so many folks about, a crowd of four …"

61

"It's going on all the time, Adamson. Nobody has found a way to stop it. Those who tried aren't available for comment any more. So I'll tell you just one more time. Forget about Durant. He's as good as gone."

Adamson's face went gray with shock. He stood there, crushed, trying to fight his way out of his depression. Joyce moved to him and placed a hand on his arm.

"It's the truth, Pa. That's the way the town is run. Nobody even bothers to argue against the top men."

"Then what in blazes are you doin' in a stinkhole like this, girl? This the kind of town you picked for yourself? And him, what's he doin', puttin' up with hellhole capers like that?"

Cherry blew out a mouthful of smoke. "I live, Adamson. I mind my own business and I let sleeping dogs lie. Nobody bothers me and I don't bother anybody else."

"How do you earn a dollar, mister?"

Cherry spread his hands. "With these and a pack of cards, Adamson. Maybe it's not the most honorable way to make a living, but it's done fine by me …"

Adamson snorted in disgust. "A gambler!" He shook his head. "My place was never suitable for her and I guess now I know why." His shoulders sagged and he looked terribly tired. He put his gun back in his holster and for a time looked to be about to change his mind. Then he straightened, fixed Joyce with a sad-eyed look and added, "Look after yourself, girl. I evidently can do no more for you."

Tears sprang up in Joyce's eyes and she turned to Cherry, silently pleading for help. Cherry gave her a frown, drew in his breath and muttered, "There's no chance."

"They'll kill him, Dane," she insisted. "He doesn't know what he's getting into."

Ben Adamson walked to the fence and hesitated, then he opened the gate, went into the night, his head bowed. Joyce grasped at Dane Cherry's arm.

"Please Dane, stop him. I'll do anything for you, I swear it."

Cherry let his eyes sweep down over her comely body. His desire for her had always been a troublesome thing, but he had held out hope that before long she would give herself to him.

He glanced back to where Adamson was walking and muttered something to himself. He thought about the town and the men he was up against. He'd always calculated the odds carefully, and realized there might be a chance to win out. If they got Durant out of jail, Joyce would be free to go anywhere with him. Adamson and his cattle would not be a barrier to that, because the herd was of no interest to Joyce or himself. He had taken enough money out of this town to set himself up comfortably in another area, and lately he had come to realize that more than a few people in this town were taking a critical interest in his activities, Traversi for one.

He called out, "Adamson, hold on!"

Ben Adamson turned, frowning. Joyce kissed Cherry gratefully on the side of the face and he moved away, checking his gun as he went. Reaching the rancher, he said:

"Is Durant that important to you, Adamson?"

"Yes."

"Then we'll give it a try. But by hell we'll do it my way and in my time. Right?"

"You'll go all the way?"

Cherry nodded grimly. "Being a damned fool, I guess I will. For the moment there's no need to hurry. We'll wait till the saloon closes and things settle down. It'll be an hour or so yet so we'll wait inside in the dark."

Adamson looked doubtfully at him. "Why, Cherry, do you think the gamble will pay off?"

"I've got a stake in it now," Cherry said and left it at that. He returned to Joyce and put his arms about her, holding her close. Joyce did not respond as eagerly as he would have liked and he was conscious that she was watching her father closely, still worried for him. So what? Her body felt good against his own and the scent of her hair excited him. Another town, another life, it'd suit him fine. He eased Joyce away, unlocked the door and let Adamson and his daughter go ahead of him. When he closed the door and got his last look at the town's main street, he began to make his plans.

Sheriff Red Traversi pushed open the jailhouse door and hurled a drunken, blubbering and bruised Bo Strawbridge inside. Directly behind him, Deputy Lem Edey dragged an unconscious Bede Strawbridge by the back of his coat and pitched him into the middle of the room. Scowling, he crossed to the desk and picked up a ring of keys, selected one and went to the end cell. He opened the door as Traversi came up behind him and shoved Bo Strawbridge into it. Edey then dragged Bo's brother to the cell, and after dropping him inside, slammed the door shut.

"One damn peep out of either of you Strawbridges, and I'll shut you up proper," he growled and threw the cell keys onto the desk top.

Red Traversi stopped at Blake Durant's cell and eyed him curiously for a moment before he said, "Comfortable, drifter?"

Blake returned his look but didn't reply. Traversi chuckled and returned to the front door. He studied the street before he said, "Best stay here with them, Lem. I'll do the rounds on my own."

Outside, the sound of hammering echoed through the night's peace. Traversi removed his hat and ruffled his hair with both hands before he went off, walking with the gait of a man who had experienced a hard day. Yet despite his evident tiredness, he found himself thinking again of the Adamson woman and the intruder who'd knocked him out with a gun butt and left a gash in his scalp.

Traversi went down the street until he came to the cleared space between the livery stable entrance and the side of the saloon. He stopped to watch three men putting up the gallows. They regarded him calmly while they kept working. Traversi gave them a nod of approval before he went on to the saloon. He climbed the outside stairs and walked along the back verandah until he came to the room Joyce Adamson had used for the last three months. Traversi opened the door, walked in and lit the lamp. It took him only a few minutes to discover that her travelling bag and some clothes were missing.

He rummaged through the bottles on her dressing table, sniffing a few of them appreciatively. The perfumes and rouge reminded him of her and he could remember the roundness of her body. He didn't for a moment doubt that he would soon claim her. But what the hell would he do with her father? If Adamson bucked him and put up a fight over his cattle, then drastic measures would have to be taken. He expected that this would complicate his association with the girl, but very few affairs in Red Traversi's life hadn't been complicated.

He was confident that he could handle the matter. Going out, he locked the door behind him and put Joyce's key into his shirt pocket. He returned to the yard and was walking back in the direction of the main street when he heard a shot.

FIVE

THE TROUBLE WITH WOMENFOLK

Dane Cherry waited until Red Traversi disappeared into the saloon laneway before he urged Ben Adamson to hurry along the opposite boardwalk. Leading the way, Cherry moved stealthily through the street's shadows until he was directly opposite the jailhouse. He stopped and made a deep study of the building before he decided on his plan of attack.

"Edey's a careful jasper, Adamson. And he isn't lacking in fight when somebody stands on his toes. Blood might have to be spilled."

Adamson nodded. "But they're gonna hang an innocent man, aren't they? That makes them murderers."

"Guess it does. First thing we've got to do is draw him out of there. See the window?"

Adamson nodded grimly while he brought his gun out of his holster.

"Get under it," Cherry said. "I'll work up to the other side of the building. When I fire a shot, be ready to rush Edey as he comes out. If he goes out the back way, you'll have to tackle him on your own. Don't think of him as a lawman or it'll be the last thought you'll ever have."

Cherry ran a hand across his face. His eyes took on a cold, brutal gleam which surprised Adamson. He now realized that Cherry was in no way worried about having to kill.

He said, "Maybe we can stop him without having to kill him. I'd prefer it that way."

"Give him a blink's start and you'll be left with lead in you," Cherry said and went off, walking faster now. When he crossed the street farther up, Adamson shuffled to the other side himself and slid into the shadows of the jailhouse laneway. His heart was pounding and sweat glistened on his heavily lined face. His hands were shaking. He cursed himself for a fool and tried to gain some measure of control over himself. But in the darkness, there seemed to be accusing eyes. He wiped the sweat from his face and bit on his bottom lip.

Time dragged, then Ben Adamson began to hear distant noises and his nervousness increased. When Cherry's shot broke into the stillness, he jolted upright, feeling relief rush into him. The door of the jailhouse opened and Adamson heard the thump of boots on the boardwalk.

Then a voice which he took to be Cherry's startled him. "Here, Deputy, quick!"

Ben Adamson waited for Edey to hurry off but no further sound disturbed the night. A full minute passed.

Then Adamson heard the stomp of footsteps down the boardwalk at the other end of town and he cursed to himself. Soon a whole army of Traversi supporters might appear and converge on them. Durant would remain a prisoner.

Ben Adamson stepped around the corner of the building beside the jailhouse, gun in hand. He saw Edey wheeling to confront him in the dark doorway.

"You damn old …"

His words were cut off by the explosion of a gun up the boardwalk. Edey's gun bucked and Adamson felt the graze of a bullet across his shoulder. Then Edey was staggering. He hit the wall with one shoulder and bounced back, turning to look for the person who'd shot him from behind. When he saw Dane Cherry coming on the run, Edey bucked upright. His gun was lifting when a second bullet slammed into his chest and punched him back into the doorway. He grabbed at the door edge, missed it and fell inside the office on his face.

Dane Cherry grabbed a horrified Ben Adamson and pushed him inside. He said, "Get Durant out and head for the back street." Cherry remained in the doorway, watching the street. The sound of someone running grew louder. Adamson snatched up the keys and opened Durant's cell, then hurried to the back door. Cherry was firing rapidly into the street and the sound of running footsteps died.

Blake Durant came out of his cell, crossed to the desk and picked up his gunbelt. He paused to look at Cherry, but Cherry, glancing back, snapped, "Move, damn you! We don't have all night."

Blake went on studying him. Then Bo Strawbridge called from his cell, "Durant, damn you, don't leave us here. Give me the keys! Get this damn cell open!"

Blake eyed the big man. For the last hour he had been talking with Bo Strawbridge, while Bede, looking like he'd run into the front end of a moving freighter, had said nothing. Blake liked Bo Strawbridge. Strawbridge was what the frontier made of a lot of men, a cowhand always on the fringe of trouble, a man making his way as best he could, getting rid of his frustrations in saloon

71

brawls and sometimes gunfights. He was the kind who would never amount to much because he had no ambition. Blake took the keys from Ben Adamson and tossed them through the bars to Bo.

By then Dane Cherry was running down the front street again, cursing the fact that the Strawbridge brothers had recognized him. It was clear to him now, thanks to Adamson and Durant, that this town was closed to him. He went into the street's shadows with Red Traversi's bullets seeking him out.

In the jailhouse, Ben Adamson was deeply troubled. Blake Durant, despite the threat over his head, seemed reluctant to quit the jailhouse and he appeared to be disturbed over the deputy's death.

"Come on, Durant," the old rancher urged. "It's done now. It was them or you."

The truth of this did nothing to relieve Durant's feeling of guilt. Even while confined in the cell, listening to the hammering from the gallows platform, he had at no stage given up hope that the top men in town would come to their senses. The injustice of his jailing didn't worry him unduly. By morning, the Judge's feelings would certainly have cooled down. Commonsense would undoubtedly prevail, he was positive of that.

But now, with a lawman killed ...

He said, "You go on."

"No, not without you, Durant. Maybe you haven't learned all you should about this bunch. They're killers and they've got the whole town under their control. Traversi is a killer, just as that deputy was."

Footsteps sounded just down the street boardwalk and Ben Adamson's imploring look finally forced Blake to walk to the back door. Bo Strawbridge had got the cell door open and was hurrying out with his brother. He stopped suddenly and turned to Blake.

"The old man's right, Durant. You best get to hell outa here in a hurry. Don't fret over Edey's killing. That had to come sooner or later and nobody will mourn him, take my word for it—"

Bo and Bede Strawbridge went into the night. Blake closed the back door and jumped to the ground. He was following Ben Adamson into the depth of the yard when the sound of somebody pounding across the floor inside came clearly to them.

"Come on for hell's sake," Adamson said urgently. "You want to be hanged in the morning?"

Blake gave him no argument. The back door opened and room light slashed out. Then Red Traversi started to punch off shots in their direction. Blake broke into a run and went into the back street shadows. They had gone only fifty yards or so with shouts rising from the belly of the town, when Dane Cherry, hatless, appeared before them.

"Go ahead, Adamson," Cherry said. "Wait at my place for me."

Cherry pushed Ben Adamson down the street and went back to take a stand at the end of the jailhouse laneway. When Blake Durant walked on, he heard the tall, good-looking gambler firing off shots. Durant, reluctant to leave a man fighting for him, nevertheless responded to Adamson's urging and followed the old man to Cherry's cabin, where Joyce waited. Joyce had just been introduced to Durant and was regarding him curiously when Cherry returned.

"Lost my damned hat and couldn't go back for it," he mumbled. "That puts the finger on me."

He stood outside, prodding bullets into his gun and muttering to himself. Then, straightening suddenly, he added, "We'd best clear out of here. There's only one place for us to go now, until we can get horses and get to blazes out of this town. Wait outside."

Blake Durant gave him no argument and Joyce moved out, her father following. Blake Durant studied the street, frowning. He was a man who shielded his loneliness as he did all his feelings. There had been moments in his life when he had been ruthless, with himself and with others. He

74

heard boards being ripped up inside and a few moments later Cherry appeared, stuffing a leather pouch into his shirt. Cherry snapped a look at him and said:

"Okay, let's get out of here. As soon as Traversi finds my hat, he'll add up some facts and come for my hide. Damn me, I could do without this night."

Cherry led the way into the front street. After carefully checking it out and seeing a crowd gathering outside the jailhouse, he stole off through the deep shadows at the end of town. It took them only three minutes to reach another slanted side street up which Cherry went at a half-run. They came to a small cottage set back in a well-kept yard. Cherry went straight to the door, tried the knob and found the door unlocked. Easing it open, he went in to find a tall, dark-haired slender woman turning slowly away from a wall cabinet, a glass in her hand. Her dark eyes flashed.

"What do you want, Cherry?" she asked sharply.

Dane Cherry showed his gun. "Take it easy, Marie, and nobody will worry you much." He motioned for the others to enter the room. He closed the door behind them, then he pulled the curtains across both small windows and turned down the lamp. All the while Marie glared at the intruders.

"What do you want? Who are you? This is my home and I don't want any of you here. Get out!"

Cherry walked to her and pushed her into a seat. "This is Marie," he said. "Traversi has a claim on her and she's always been satisfied with that, so don't trust her."

"You louse, Cherry!" Marie tried to get to her feet but Cherry kept her down, then he held the gun inches from her face.

"Marie, hear me out before you start making a noise. Edey's dead. I killed him and in a short time Traversi will know it was me. So he'll tear this whole town down, looking for me. Only he isn't gonna find me, not tonight. This man is Ben Adamson. Traversi means to steal cattle from him. You know his daughter, Joyce."

Marie looked scathingly at Joyce Adamson. "Yes, I know her all right, with her fine ways and pretences. And I know you, Cherry. So get out before I make enough noise to bring the whole town here."

"No noise," Cherry said, a heavy threat in his voice. Marie suddenly leaned back and tossed her drink into his face. Cherry merely grinned as he wiped the liquor away with his handkerchief.

"This fellow, Marie, is Blake Durant. He was being held for murder and was sentenced to hang in the morning."

Marie's gaze moved to take in Durant, as he said, "I don't know that we should stay here, Cherry."

Cherry waved a hand. "Don't worry about Marie. She'll do as I say or take the consequences."

"There'll be no consequences, Cherry," Durant said and the gambler straightened, fixing him with a fierce look.

"Look, Durant, don't try to ride herd on me. Thanks to you, I'm in about as much trouble as I feel inclined to handle. Adamson begged me to help him get you out of that jailhouse and if I hadn't killed Edey he'd be a dead man himself right now. So settle down and let me handle this my way."

Blake Durant glanced at Ben Adamson who stood tight-lipped and worried, looking across the room. Adamson nodded in agreement with Cherry's words, adding, "I couldn't see any other way for it, Durant. I won't stand by and let them hang you in the morning. I'm sorry as I can be about the deputy, but Edey gave us no chance to talk. We meant to knock him out, no more."

"He's no loss," Cherry put in. Marie suddenly lunged for him, but he caught her arms and pushed her back.

"Red will kill you for this!" Marie shouted. "No matter where you go, he'll find you. Lem was his closest friend."

"Sure. Lem kept good men from putting a bullet in Red," Dane Cherry said. "Now shut down. I need time to think."

Durant moved closer to Marie and lounged against the wall. Dane Cherry frowned a little, then he turned from Durant and took Joyce to the other side of the room. After studying her thoughtfully for some time, he said:

"I've done what you asked and now I'm holding you to your word, Joyce. We'll get out of this somehow, then I'm washing my hands of these other two. You and me—we'll go together. Right?"

Joyce couldn't hide her disturbed feelings. She looked quickly at her father who frowned but said nothing. Joyce's gaze went to Blake Durant then, the man who had caused all this trouble. Earlier she had decided that he looked like a man capable of handling his own affairs confidently. There was a strangeness about him. He was different from other men and she didn't understand the feelings he aroused in her. She was confused. He wasn't nearly as handsome as Dane Cherry, but there was a clean-cut ruggedness about him that was appealing.

"But what about Pa?" she asked.

"What about him? You left him a year ago and he came to town riding on the back of trouble. To hell with him. I've helped him all I feel obliged to do. Now it's you and me I've got to think about, plus getting us both out of this town in one piece."

Ben Adamson regarded Cherry sourly. "Nobody asked you to do more than what you've already

78

done, Cherry," he said. "I'm obliged for the help and I don't intend to stand in my daughter's way in any regard. But don't try to ride me down any more. I've never let any man do that."

Cherry waved the old man's words away and moved to the door. He pressed his ear against the timber and listened intently. Despite his air of calmness, Blake Durant saw a shadow of deep concern move across the gambler's face. Then Durant watched the Adamson girl, remembering what Adamson had told him about her … a young woman who had lost her mother and had been unable to get the right kind of guidance in her maturing years from a father who, because of pressure of work and business, had too little time to devote to her.

He found Joyce disturbingly attractive.

Cherry began to pace the room thoughtfully. Blake decided, for the moment at least, to fall into line with anything Cherry suggested. It was evident that Cherry knew this town and enough tricks of the trade to be able to make the right moves. But once he was out of this mess, Blake Durant meant to make his own decisions.

Suddenly Blake and Cherry swung around as they heard a noise outside. Cherry strode to the lamp and turned down the wick. He then went to the window, drew back the curtains and looked out. Durant dropped his hand onto his gun and in the murky light Marie studied him intently.

Cherry grunted something, dropped the curtains back in place, drew his gun. He said, "There's a bunch of men at the top of this lane. Everybody stay quiet. This is the last place Traversi should come, but you never know with him."

Marie dropped her gaze when Cherry looked her way. Cherry, distracted again by a louder noise from outside, hurried back to the window. As he pulled the curtain back, Marie jumped to her feet and hurled the glass. The glass hit the middle of the window and smashed it.

Cherry wheeled about, his face savage with anger, his gun leveling on her.

Marie threw back her head and shouted, "Red! They're here, Red!"

Cherry took two quick steps towards her but Blake Durant stepped in front of him and shouldered him back. "Leave her be, Cherry. She didn't invite us here so she owes us nothing."

Cherry scowled at him. "Damn you, Durant, do you think we're playing games with that crowd? Traversi's a killer. He won't show any mercy if he gets his hands on us."

"Then we'll fight like men, mister. And that means we leave womenfolk be."

"To hell with you!" Cherry tried to sweep Blake Durant aside, but the drifter stood his ground, his bulk too much for Cherry to budge. The gun in Durant's hand, plus the fierce defiance in his eyes, caused Cherry to have second thoughts. Before either of them could take it further, Traversi's voice boomed out.

"Get down, Marie!"

Bullets began to smash into the side of the cottage. Ben Adamson grabbed Joyce and forced her down to the floor. Marie rushed for the door but Cherry dived at her and knocked her to the side. After a brief struggle he subdued her and although the young woman continued to lash out furiously at him, Cherry finally pinned her and kept her face pushed against the dusty floorboards.

The bullets began to shake the door and front walls. Durant said, "We have to get out of here, Cherry. It's up to you and me to make the first break and give cover. Adamson, can you look after the women?"

"Sure. But hell, Durant, I'm in this to my ears, same as you."

"Just watch the women," Durant said and crawled across the floor to where Cherry still held the struggling Marie. Durant touched the gambler on the shoulder and when Cherry looked around at him, he said, "What's out back?"

"Open country."

"Then we'll let Adamson make a break for it. You take one window."

"Go to hell!" Cherry snapped.

Blake pointed his gun at Cherry. "Mister, Adamson and his daughter are getting whatever chance we can make for them. You and I can hold them off here."

Cherry's stare slashed at Durant. "Look, I don't want any part of you. I think it was a damn fool idea getting you out of Traversi's jailhouse in the first place. You just do whatever you like and leave me be."

"What I like right now, mister, is giving other people a chance. Let go of her."

Marie regarded Durant coolly, plainly not believing that he wanted to help her. But Durant's calm look remained on her and she couldn't bring herself to abuse him. She drove her elbows into Cherry's stomach and smiled when he let out a grunt.

Cherry grabbed her by the shoulder and she gasped in pain. Then Durant's hand fastened on Cherry's wrist and slowly the pressure of his grip made the gambler release Marie again.

"You can buy a heap of trouble acting like that," Durant said. He spoke slowly, hoping his words would be sufficient warning and that Cherry would know when to stop.

The shooting had stopped. Now Red Traversi's voice boomed out: "Marie, you all right?"

Marie squirmed from under Cherry and lifted her head. "Come on in, Red. They're scared. You can get them easily."

"Shut down, you!" Cherry told her and pushed her head hard onto the boards.

Blake Durant couldn't help her now. He had risen to his feet and pulled the door open. Looking out, he saw a group of five men crouched up the laneway. The closest was about thirty yards away. As Cherry had said, the back yard was open country.

Durant ducked back when a barrage of bullets slammed into the front of the house. He said, "Adamson, put out the lamp. Then come up behind me. When I start firing, take your daughter out the back way and keep going. Don't stop for anybody or anything."

Blake Durant stepped outside, picked out his target and opened fire. The closest of the five men immediately backed off. Durant kept firing until he heard Adamson go down the front of the cottage with Joyce close behind. Then he stepped back inside and partly closed the door. Cherry was against the inside wall, with Marie held close to him.

Durant said, "Okay, you two next."

But Cherry defied him. "That trick worked once, Durant, but it won't again. Make your own arrangements and I'll make mine. I know this town and I'll find a hiding place in it. West of here, about ten miles out, there's a canyon. Beyond it is a place called Eagle's Rock. There are caves throughout that section. Find one, stay there, and wait for me."

"I can't leave you in this fight on your own," Durant said.

Cherry laughed scornfully. "Durant, I'd rather be on my own than tied in with you. You've got your chance—take it because you mightn't get another one. I've got Marie, so Traversi will have to toe the line with me."

Durant thought about the situation while bullets continued to rock the walls of the house. He knew that time was fast running out for all of them. By now Adamson would be at the fence.

He said, "I think you're loco, but you leave me no choice."

"So run, damn you!"

Blake waited for the shooting to die down, then he slipped out through the doorway again. He held his fire. In the deep shadows down the side of the building he went noiselessly. But just as he was turning towards the back of the cottage, a figure loomed up before him. Blake saw a gun gleam in the moonlight. He brought his left fist crashing down on the man's shoulder. As the man's legs buckled under him, Durant's right fist swung up and made contact with the point of the jaw. The man let out a groan and slumped into the dust. Blake stepped over him, then backed off. When he reached the fence he stopped. Ahead of him he could see the gun hands coming in closer, spread out for a fight.

Then the fleeting figures of two people passed by the corner of the cottage.

He heard Cherry call, "Traversi, I'm going through you. Try to stop me and Marie gets it."

Blake cursed under his breath and climbed over the fence. Adamson and Joyce were waiting. Blake snapped, "I told you to keep going."

"We'll go now, Durant."

Even as the rancher spoke, guns burst into life in front of the cottage. Marie let out a tortured scream. Then Blake saw Cherry pitch her body forward and break into a run. The gambler headed down the laneway through a gauntlet of six-gun lead. He clutched his shoulder and staggered, but continued on. When Cherry reached the end of the laneway and ran from sight, Blake pushed Adamson into a stumbling run.

"Head for the livery stable and get your horses. I'll cover."

Ben Adamson, having seen Marie stumble and fall, gave him no argument this time. With Joyce running to keep up, they went into the back street. When Durant arrived they had saddles on two horses. Adamson stood guard over a perspiring, frightened stable attendant while Durant saddled Sundown. Then, riding hard, they tore out of town by way of the back street.

SIX

"FIND CHERRY!"

Red Traversi's anger was like a striking snake inside him. In the light of the lantern brought from the cottage, he held Marie in his strong arms. Her eyes were closed and her face was already gray. But there was some semblance of life still inside her.

"Get her a drink, quick!"

Reg Weedon hurried to the cottage and returned with a bottle of whiskey that he handed to Traversi. Feeding whiskey into Marie's mouth, Traversi then studied her anxiously for signs of life. But the whiskey ran scarlet back through her lips and her head dropped to the side of his forearm. His curse was bitter as he placed her on the ground.

For a long time Red Traversi stood there, remembering the wild spirit which had made Marie interesting to him. Some of their tender moments together came to him. He drew in a slow, deep breath and faced the other four.

"Take her inside. Lay her down right, then leave her be. I'll tend to her myself later when there's more time. Right now I want you to rouse the whole damn town. I want everybody in the streets. I want Cherry."

Reg Weedon, sensing that the slightest delay would send Traversi into a fit of temper, bent down and lifted Marie from the ground. He carried her limp body into the cottage and put her on her bed. Returning, he stood in the doorway and checked his gun. Traversi had sent the others running for help. They had just reached the front street when the sound of hoof beats rose from the back street.

Snarling angrily, Traversi called out, "Get your horses. We'll run 'em down. I want you to kill the whole damn lot of 'em!"

He charged off, the loss of Marie cutting deep into him. Weedon fetched Traversi's horse for him and then Traversi was holding Dane Cherry's hat high for the gathered men to see.

"A hundred dollars for the man who shoots the guts out of the scum whose head fits this hat. Weedon, stay here. Get whatever help you need, but see that those cattle don't shift outa town."

Traversi walked to his horse and swung up. With a cold look at the men who had come to his assistance, he hit his horse into a run.

A fly lighted on the back of Durant's hand as he listened to the sound of water running over rocks. Around him were the gray bones of a long-dead tree. Sundown stood still, peering into the sun-up's yellow-pink light. Ben Adamson, after the long, hard ride from town, looked weary and uncertain.

Durant made his decision. "Cherry suggested we go to a place called Eagle's Rock, but the girl heard him mention it. I think we should avoid the place at all costs."

"The girl was shot," Adamson put in.

"But maybe she wasn't killed. Cherry went off and left her behind. If she lived to talk then she's put Traversi onto our trail." Durant turned his gaze onto Joyce, remembering her connection with Dane Cherry. "It's up to you, Miss Adamson. No matter how he did it, Cherry helped get us out of town and he saved me from a hanging."

Ben Adamson studied his daughter's face and then sighed. "We sure got ourselves into one hell of a pickle, didn't we? My cattle are still back there. Without them, I might as well be dead. Damned if I'm gonna leave 'em there."

Joyce held Durant's steady gaze. It was growing warmer, with the sun rising through the timber and shining on their faces. Joyce shivered and touched her disarranged her, wondering about Durant and angry at herself for it. The man meant nothing to her. On the ride from town he had been methodical in everything he did, apparently certain that whatever he decided was right for them. He had never allowed any argument and she and her father had followed him blindly.

Now she said. "I gave him my word when he helped Pa raid the jailhouse, Mr. Durant. I said I'd wait for him and go with him."

Durant nodded his acceptance of this but his cool look brought a flush of color to Joyce's face. She faced him, drawing herself up a little, a picture of uncertainty despite the forthright answer she had given him.

He said: "I suggest we wait here, water the horses and get some rest. We've put a good deal of distance between us and the town and likely we've gained a big break on anybody following. Cherry will be along and he should be able to pick up our tracks."

With that Blake Durant led the way through the trees and down to the creek's edge where he came out of the saddle. Before Joyce or her father could unsaddle their horses, Durant had Sundown hitched in shade and was gathering wood for a fire. Soon he had a smokeless fire going. When the water in a black pot was on the boil, he added coffee grains.

Minutes later Joyce and her father were seated out of the fire's heat drinking coffee. Then Ben Adamson broke the silence.

"What actually happened to the girl, Durant?"

Blake shook his head. "It was too dark to see properly."

"You were closer than us," Adamson persisted. "All we saw was Cherry holding her up as a shield. Then guns started to go off."

Blake sipped at his coffee and looked at the fire. "Hard to say who started the last bout of shooting. It might have been Traversi or it could have been Cherry."

Adamson cleared his throat and hunched forward. "If it was Cherry, he gave the girl no chance."

Joyce frowned at him. "What are you trying to say, Pa?"

Adamson shrugged. "Ain't sayin' it any way, girl. Just wonderin'."

Joyce turned to Durant. "You both think Dane was responsible for her death, don't you? That's a terrible accusation to make. And unfair."

"It was too dark to see anything definite, Miss Adamson," Durant said quietly. "But he had no right to use her that way."

"What was the alternative?" she asked hotly. "Should he have stayed there to get killed?"

Blake's look hardened a little and he began to understand how difficult it must have been for Adamson to live with Joyce on his ranch after the death of her mother.

"No," he said. "I didn't expect him to stay and get killed. But I didn't expect him to throw her into a wild gunfight either. I see him again I'll put it to him personally."

"You will?" Joyce said, her voice rising again. "Perhaps you'll also forget what he's done for you?"

Blake shook his head. "I won't forget that. But let's face something. He wasn't out to do me a favor—he had a deal on. Cherry is maybe a little bit too keen on deals for my liking."

Blake rose, kicked some dust over the fire and returned his coffee mug to Sundown's saddle. He stood then, his eyes going beyond the creek, searching.

Adamson walked away from the fire too and washed his mug in the slow-running creek. Coming back, he found Joyce looking moodily at her leather-chafed hands. He said, "Don't argue with Durant. He got into this for my sake. I won't have him harped at by you."

Joyce looked defiantly at her father and for a moment seemed about to continue her argument.

Then she apparently changed her mind and got to her feet. She stood looking into the distance, her face dark with rage. Ben Adamson shook his head sadly and tried to remember her mother as she had been at Joyce's age, spirited, stubborn, hot-headed and careless with her arguments. Finally, however, she had become tolerant with age. Perhaps, he told himself, it would be like that with Joyce too.

He walked to his horse and patted its head, then he sat down on a tree stump and took out his gun. He hunched over, weighing the gun in each hand. The morning silence settled comfortably about him and he cleared his mind of all thoughts.

Dane Cherry came up the creek bank right on noon. When Joyce saw him, she was overcome with delight. But then, as she walked to meet him, she saw the blood on his shoulder.

"Dane!" she cried out.

Cherry lifted his head. His face carried the weariness of a man who had ridden the night and half a day, alone, tormented by pain. His dull gaze settled on her and a thin smile worked across his thin-lipped mouth.

Cherry stopped just before the fire and looked bleakly up to where Adamson and Blake Durant stood in the shade of the cottonwoods. His face gave no hint to his feelings. Joyce moved beside his horse as he came down from the saddle. She took the reins from him and led the horse off. Cherry braced himself on wide-planted feet and said angrily:

"This isn't Eagle Rock, Durant. Did you figure to run out on me?"

Blake shook his head. "We knew you'd pick up our trail. We also knew that if Marie lived to talk, Traversi would have gone seeking us out at Eagle Rock."

Cherry sneered. "I've already taken care of Traversi, no thanks to you," he growled. "He tracked me down just on sunup and I led him away into the hills. It was only by chance that I picked up your trail."

"It doesn't matter now anyway," Ben Adamson put in. "You're here and we're here. What I've got to worry about now is getting my daughter to some place safe. After that I'm gonna get my cattle back."

Cherry's face held a smug smile. "I told you before that you can forget your cattle, Adamson. As for Joyce, she's my responsibility now. By the time Traversi gets onto my trail, I'll have her a long way from here."

Cherry moved to Joyce and placed a hand on her shoulder. She shifted away, regarding him critically. "Did Marie die?" she asked bluntly.

94

Cherry frowned. Then he shrugged. "I don't know."

"If she did, Dane, was it your fault?"

Cherry's face clouded and his mouth thinned. He swung his look to Durant and Adamson. "Did they say that?"

Joyce licked at her lips. Then Blake Durant pushed himself away from the tree trunk and made his way to the edge of the fire. He poked the ashes with a stick and turned to Cherry.

"Who fired the first shot, you or Traversi?"

Cherry stood sullenly before him for a long moment. Then he growled, "Traversi, damn you! I meant to get Marie past them. I didn't think Traversi would risk hitting her. But he did."

Blake nodded and looked down at the fire again. Ben Adamson, watching Cherry shrewdly, suddenly grunted a curse that made Joyce glare at him. Adamson ignored her searching look and walked slowly to Blake.

"What now, Durant?"

Blake shook his head and looked up at the high slopes that shaded the creek. "We've still got to get your cattle back, Adamson. We won't get them sitting here."

Adamson's eyes brightened. "You're still in it? You'd go back there with me?"

"I don't like to leave things undone."

95

"You're both loco," Cherry said tightly. "Traversi will hunt us down and if he finds us there'll be a bloodbath. Marie was his girl. He'll blame us for getting her killed."

Joyce gasped. "But you just said that you didn't know if she died or not. Are you lying to me?"

Cherry fixed her with a fierce look. "She was hit front on, damn it! I haven't met the woman yet who could take a six-gun bullet there and live. So she's dead and nobody's lying, certainly not me." He stepped back, dragging his hand through his curly hair. "Which means Traversi and his owl hoot mob will be out in force. I gave them the slip at sunup but they'll find my tracks and come here. I reckon we've got about an hour, so make up your minds. You coming or not?"

Joyce looked anxiously at her father. "Pa?"

Adamson held her look for a moment before he shook his head. "I must get my cattle back, Joyce. If I lose them, I've got nothing to live for."

She moved to him and placed a hand on his hairy forearm. "Pa, you still have me. Come with us. Dane will know where to go. We can start again."

Adamson frowned and shifted away from her. "Can't, girl," he said. "There's my ranch and the lifetime of work I've put in it. Maybe it ain't much of a place but it's mine. It's got my brand on it and your ma is buried under it. I can't ride away from that and I can't let thievin' scum take my cattle. If I walk away from this I'll never be able to live with myself."

Joyce pursed her lips thoughtfully and suddenly said, "Then why can't we go to another town and find an honest law officer? We could get him to investigate the mattter for us." Her eyes brightened. "Why not, Pa?"

"Because that would be a waste of time," Dane Cherry put in. "If the law did come and make an investigation, they'd find themselves listening to a town full of liars and cowards. Traversi would have no trouble convincing them that he's done no wrong, especially when a sentenced man broke jail and when a girl was killed, along with a deputy. Can't you work out the story Traversi would put up?"

"He's right," Blake Durant said. "We've got to do it ourselves." He turned to Cherry and his voice was matter-of-fact when he said, "Where does Traversi's outfit keep their money? Not in the bank, I don't suppose."

Cherry shook his head. "Nope. Traversi don't trust banks. But there's a big safe back of the jailhouse. I reckon he's got his hoard there."

Durant gave a slow nod of his head. "Then that's the answer," he muttered,

"Rob him?" Adamson asked, frowning.

"Why not? It'd be nigh impossible for us to run those cattle out of town. So we won't bother to do that. We take money to cover their cost."

Ben Adamson thought about it and smiled. "By hell, you're right. If we were told right, Traversi's been bleeding that town dry for months. He'd have plenty of money stashed away. We break in, take what we want and get to hell out. They don't even have to know we came back."

Joyce, studying Dane Cherry thoughtfully, saw his eyes cloud up with thought as he looked from one man to the other. When he straightened, sucking in a deep breath, she saw a rush of excitement take hold of him.

Then Blake Durant said, "What about it, Cherry? We can use you and your knowledge of that town."

Cherry scowled at him. "You've just got to be foolin', Durant. I wouldn't go back there for anything."

"Not even for the girl?" Durant pushed at him.

Joyce regarded Durant angrily. "That's unfair, Mr. Durant."

"Is it?" Blake said. "The right kind of man would want to help his woman's father. And your father needs a great deal of help right now. I think you should begin to consider him a little. He spent a lifetime trying to look after you and it's not his fault that you got dissatisfied with your lot."

Joyce colored and looked guiltily at her father. Adamson said nothing. But Dane Cherry stepped towards Durant, his face tight.

"Now see here Durant. I don't reckon this is any of your business. Damn you, mister, I ..."

"Don't damn me, Cherry," Blake cut in. "I have an obligation to you, sure, but that doesn't give you any rights with me. What I know of you so far I don't much approve of. The way you get your money sickens me. The way you strut annoys me. And the way you wheedle and scheme to get what you want puts bile in my belly. Either you do a decent thing for once in your life or you get to hell out of here."

Durant's angry outburst left the others stunned. Cherry stood there as if somebody had slapped his face, then he swung to the side and his hand slashed down for his gun. But before his Colt was clear of the holster, Blake Durant's gun was in his hand, leveled, and the look in his eyes spelled only death.

Cherry's hand froze on his gun butt. Blake Durant watched him closely. Only when Cherry's hand dropped in submission did his own hand go back to holster his Colt.

"We'll leave it at that," Durant said. "Now climb on your horse and get going. And don't stop."

Cherry hesitated a moment, then he turned and walked to his horse. Joyce took a tentative step towards him but her father placed a hand on her shoulder and said:

"I need you girl. This last time. Don't leave me."

Moisture gleamed in Joyce's eyes.

Cherry stopped and studied her critically but when she made no move to come to him, he said, "It's loco. They'll both get killed. Traversi owns the whole town and they'll be primed up to kill."

Blake Durant said, "We know what's ahead of us, Cherry. Move off and leave well enough alone."

Joyce still looked uncertainly at each of them, her father's hand firm on her shoulder. She put her hand over his and said, "I'm sorry, Dane."

Cherry shrugged and turned away. But a spasm of pain started again in his shoulder when he took hold of the pommel. He grunted and then swore under his breath. Joyce moved away from her father quickly and went to Cherry.

"Let me fix your wound first, Dane."

Cherry nodded. "Wouldn't mind," he muttered. He dropped the reins and came back to where Durant stood. "Guess you got to stand my smell a while longer, Durant."

"Why not?" Durant returned. "You don't count in any way." He walked away, stopped near Adamson and said, "We know the town well enough. If we get back there by tomorrow night, riding in easy stages, our horses will hold up for us. Under cover of dark we shouldn't have any trouble getting into the jail-house. You know anything about opening a safe?"

Ben Adamson shook his head. "Only seen one or two; didn't have any use for one at home. Hell, I never had enough loose money lying about to fill a gun chamber."

"It's easy," Cherry put in, causing Blake to turn.

"That so, Cherry?"

"Sure. I had a friend who blew up a few. You pack gunpowder sticks on the hinge side. Light the fuse and the door falls off."

"Where do we get gunpowder?" Blake asked.

Cherry grinned. "At the gunpowder store, where else?"

Blake Durant's hardening look made him grin wider. He stepped away as Joyce finished bandaging his arm and said, "Been thinking it over. Maybe I'll tag along. I been down the south country and didn't take to it much. So I guess I'll just go through Outcast County again and keep tackin' to the north. On the way I might as well throw my weight in with you fools. Then maybe Joyce will reconsider her promise to me."

Joyce smiled warmly at him. "Of course I will, Dane. Naturally things will be different if you help Pa."

"Then it's a deal," Cherry said, stepping towards his horse. This time he went into the saddle effortlessly. His brows hooded his dark eyes as he looked into the country they would have to travel. "The sooner we quit this place, the better," he muttered and heeled his horse off through the timber, Joyce following on her pony.

Ben Adamson asked, "What you reckon?"

Blake shrugged. "I don't know yet. We'll see."

"Don't trust him," Adamson said thickly. "Too many twists to him."

Blake nodded, wondering how much money was in Traversi's safe. Maybe Cherry had the same thought.

SEVEN

CONFRONTATION TRAIL

Blake Durant tried to see Joyce's face but the deepening shadows hid her expression. However, he had the distinct impression that whatever Cherry was saying to her was not impressing her much.

Durant wondered if the long day's ride had given her sufficient time to think things out. He couldn't believe she was so stupid that she didn't see beneath the veneer of Cherry's charm. The man was a clever rascal.

They had come across the vast rolling plain of sand, rock and cactus which was the northern desert and were now on the fringe of stunted pine country. The air was cool after the heat of the desert, and the silence seemed to have comfort in it, for which Durant knew Joyce would be grateful. Finally, towards sundown, they made camp.

After supper, Joyce left Cherry and crossed the campsite to her father who was stretched out near his horse. Cherry climbed to a hilltop where Blake sat watching the country about them. Squatting on his haunches, Cherry dug into the ground with a stick and whistled to himself.

Then, finally: "Durant, we got nothing going for each other, have we?"

"Very little, mister."

Anger showed in Cherry's face. "Fair enough. But you reckon two men in our state of mind should take on a town like Outcast County? You reckon one of us might break?"

"I won't," Durant told him.

Cherry grinned in the growing darkness. "Well, in ordinary circumstances, I wouldn't let any man down. But I've got the feeling that Joyce is taken with you, drifter. And I don't like it."

"I don't much care what you like or don't like, Cherry," Durant told him, almost casually.

"It's because of Joyce that I changed my mind about not tagging along," Cherry said. "I'd just hate to tack off on my own and leave you with a free rein. She's too young to understand about men like you."

It was Durant's turn to smile. "What about men like me, Cherry?"

Cherry dug up a piece of hard earth and tossed it away, then he began to widen the hole it had left. "Your kind, Durant, don't impress me at all. You drift along, trying to give the impression that you're carefree and couldn't give a damn. But you ain't like that one spit, mister. You're scared deep down."

Blake frowned.

Cherry explained quickly. "Scared of staying in one place too long, scared of letting folks get to know you too much. What kind of past have you left behind, Durant?"

"That's my business, mister."

"Women, Durant?" Cherry's eyes widened with the mocking question. He tossed the stick away and cleaned his right hand down the side of his levis. When the hand came close to his gun, his look sharpened. But Blake Durant didn't react.

"Leave it alone," Durant said after a moment. "Better that way for both of us."

There was a hint of warning in Durant's tone, but Cherry took no notice of it. Settling back, he caught his hands behind his neck and grinned up at the sky.

"I reckon there was a woman, Durant. Did she give you that fool bandanna you're wearin'?" There was amusement in Cherry's drawl.

Durant's face hardened. The twisted curl of Cherry's thin lips annoyed him now. He said, evenly, "We've been thrown together to help a man, mister. Don't make it any rougher than you have to. In an hour we'll be pushing on. I suggest that you use that time to get some rest."

Blake stood up and turned to leave, but Cherry kept at him, his voice suddenly becoming harsh. "What I mean to say, Durant, is that I want you to steer clear of Joyce. If you don't, I'll kill you. I'll find a way."

Cherry stood rock-still and defiant as Durant's stare swept over him. From the very beginning he hadn't taken to Cherry, but now he wanted to drive him into the ground, to put him in his place really hard.

He said, "There was a woman, Cherry, a pretty wonderful woman. She meant the world to me, and her memory still means everything. You mention her again, even hint at her being a part of my past, and I'll spread you all over this slope."

Cherry took a quick step back and looked uneasy for a moment. But then Durant walked away. When he got to the bottom of the slope he saw Joyce standing against a tree. The way she looked at him told him that she'd heard everything.

She said, "That was wrong of him, Mr. Durant. He had no right."

Blake shrugged. "Nothing Cherry does worries me, ma'am."

Durant had stopped and now he looked at her in a way that made her blush. She didn't know why but she felt heat rising in her face. The cool wind whipped across her body and tightened her light blouse against her breasts. She felt his gaze linger on her bosom a moment and didn't mind. It occurred to her then that this man excited her. She found herself comparing him with Dane Cherry.

"Was she beautiful?" she asked suddenly.

Durant nodded. "Very."

"Your wife?"

"We had planned to marry. It didn't come to that."

Joyce looked surprised. "She gave a man like you away?"

Blake shook his head. "She was killed. An accident."

"Oh." She shifted away from him and looked into the sky. After a moment she said, "Dane has a habit of upsetting people. I wouldn't take too much notice of what he says. He gets restless when there's no excitement. But when trouble comes, you'll find that he's reliable."

Blake heard her out and smiled tightly. "He'd better be." Then he went off to get some rest, leaving Joyce staring after him. Her father was snoring on the ground a short distance away and Dane Cherry was squatting on a log tossing stones at a dead tree stump. When Durant disappeared from sight near the horses, Joyce returned to Cherry. He looked up with a start to find her there and said:

"Where have you been?"

"Talking to Mr. Durant. I like him, Dane. Why don't you?"

Cherry sneered. "Durant ain't my type, that's all. And you keep away from him. I know what you've been thinking, that he's done so much for your pa. Well, just leave it at that. I'm not risking my neck a second time for him unless I get what's due me."

"I wish you wouldn't refer to me in that way, Dane," Joyce said angrily. "I'm not a piece of trading material."

"Maybe not. But I'll get you, Joyce—and more. Traversi has plenty of cash money and gold stashed away in the safe. So we kill two birds with the one stone. We get compensation for your pa for all his trouble and losses and I get me a slice of good currency to help you and me get settled good someplace. Won't hardly be stealing, taking money from Traversi."

Joyce looked worried. Dane Cherry had changed a great deal in these last few days. Or had he really changed? Could it be just that she'd been blind to his shortcomings and now the comparison with Blake Durant gave her a truer picture of him?

She said, "Mr. Durant said we should get some rest, Dane. I think we should."

"Sure," Cherry agreed and after a furtive glance across to where her father lay, he reached for her. But she moved away, shaking her head.

"When it's all over, Dane. Not until."

"A damn waste," he grinned, his good humor coming back suddenly.

"I have my pride," she said.

He chuckled then, enjoying her more. Now, as she made for her father's side, she knew with certainty that a great many changes would have to be made in Dane Cherry's make-up for her to keep her promise to him.

It was late afternoon when Red Traversi returned to Outcast County after two days on the trail. Alec Day and Ben Peters, who had fouled up the cattle yard raid in which Rick Eggert had been killed, trailed a few horse lengths away. Strung out behind them were seven raw-eyed, thirsty, disgruntled hired guns. Traversi had been anything but pleasant company on the long dusty ride through the foothills, across the desert and back along the low country. They had seen his temper get worse by the mile until now only Day and Peters were game to go within call of him.

Turning a corner on the long main street, Traversi suddenly reined up and flung himself out of the saddle. In two bounds he was on the boardwalk and in another stride had Bo Strawbridge by the collar. He pulled Bo off his feet and with a tremendous heave sent him smashing into the building wall. Bede Strawbridge then came rushing out of a store doorway, throwing punches at Traversi's head, but the sheriff stopped him dead in his tracks with a powerful right that landed flush on Bede's jaw. The big man merely shook his head and came back swinging. Traversi hit him twice more on the side of the jaw, but Bede retaliated with a blow over the heart. Red Traversi went reeling back. By then Bo had come off the wall, wiping blood from his chin. Traversi glanced back and saw his hired guns bunched, none of them coming in for a share of this fight.

He took a sudden step to the boardwalk's edge and when Bo came at him, pulled his gun clear and brought it crashing down on the side of his big head. Bo's feet went out from under him. Bede lunged in past his brother's falling body but Traversi flung his gun-loaded fist up and caught him in the middle of the face. Bone cracked.

Bede went down on top of Bo. Traversi then kicked both of them in the ribs, and stepping back, wiped the sweat from his face with a bandanna.

"Drag these scum back into the jailhouse," he said. "One of you go fetch Eggert and somebody find Weedon for me. By hell, this town is gonna know what's what!"

Traversi gave the moaning Bo Strawbridge a kick in the neck for good measure before he turned and strode down the boardwalk. He was pacing his office, the cell doors open, when the gun hands came in. Traversi watched them dump the unconscious brothers in the two cells, then he sat on the edge of his desk, black eyes fixed on the door.

Judge Joe Alroe Eggert came in first, tugging at his black coat ends. Traversi barked, "Well, what you been up to while I was eatin' damn ridge dust, Judge?"

Eggert stopped short of Traversi and scowled. "Seems you're in a bad mood, Red. Figure to lose some heat bawlin' me out?"

Traversi's lips curled back. "Been settin' in the saloon by the stink of you, Judge."

The judge nodded. "Yeah, I been doing that. Does that bother you, Red?" He dragged a fat cigar from his vest pocket, "Didn't find them, eh?"

"Nope. Got wind of Cherry at one stage, but he wriggled away, damn snivellin' little sneak."

"No sign of the others?"

Traversi shook his head. He was rapidly composing himself. "Only their tracks, heading for the creek country. Cherry was aimed further south, in the direction of Eagle Rock, but we lost his tracks in the desert. Spent a whole damn day lookin' out there and got nothin' but windburn. So we come back."

Eggert bit off the end of his cigar and thumbed a match alight. "Is that the end of it for you, Red?"

Their stares locked across the empty room. Then Eggert smiled. "You failed, Red. That's too bad. I don't like a man who fails."

Cold anger burned from Traversi's eyes. But he kept his temper in check. "Nobody failed. We didn't have an owl's chance out there. We should have got them here in town. You were in that ruckus at Marie's place. How come you didn't do so well?"

"I didn't figure Cherry had the guts he showed. That's a mistake we both made, Red. We didn't check out Dane Cherry well enough. We underestimated him just as we did that drifter, Durant. What we should have done was hang Durant when we had the chance. Then maybe Edey would still be alive along with that woman of yours."

"And that was my fault, Judge?" Red Traversi barked.

"You run this jailhouse, Red. They took him from here, and it was here that Edey took his Boot Hill steps. So let's have you simmer down some, eh, and get this wrangle sorted out."

Traversi swept his red hair back from his eyes and planted his hat more firmly on his head. He had meant to call Eggert down and let him know who was boss of this outfit, once and for all. But things hadn't gone his way.

"You sort it out," he said. "Weedon and his bunch failed to get the old man out in the plains. He come on through the valley during the night and they decided it was better to wait for him in town. You threw in with that, didn't you?"

"Sure," Judge Eggert admitted.

"Same as me," Traversi said easily. "But Adamson linked up with that drifter, Durant. Weedon messed a night raid with Day, your boy and Peters. Your boy was killed."

Eggert's eyes went as hard as flint. But he said nothing.

"After that Cherry bought in for some damn fool reason of his own and killed Edey. All we got was his hat. Then they blasted their way out of a trap we'd set for them and I got burned raw chasin' them in the hills."

"That's about it except for one little thing, Red," Eggert said.

Traversi waited for it, watching the cigar glow as the judge puffed.

"You weren't on hand when you had a prisoner in your keeping, Red. That prisoner had killed my boy, so you should have been real careful to keep him here so I could hang him. You failed me, Red, because you were trying to maul a woman who didn't want to have a thing to do with you. I hear you were knocked out. Cherry, maybe?"

Traversi stood still, his hands hanging slack. A gleam showed in his narrowed eyes. "Must have been him, yeah. Who else?"

"Precisely, Red," Eggert kept on. "Who else? Cherry, who was trying to win favor with Joyce Adamson. Dane Cherry, who had the freedom of this town and was tolerated by all of us—he did the greatest damage, Red, and you want to know why?"

Traversi still held his silence. A nerve jumped in his temple as his jaws clamped tight.

"Dane Cherry fooled us, Red. We didn't look deep enough into him. He isn't the dude we figured him to be. In fact, from what I've got in your absence, Dane Cherry has been cleaning up real well right under our eyes. Now why didn't we crowd him a little and make him share with us, Red? Because, once again, we spent too much time worrying about fools like those two in the cells. Now

114

the whole town is laughing at us. We've lost a lot of respect. How are we gonna get it back?"

Traversi frowned. "How the hell should I know? You're the brains—you tell me."

"I will, Red. What we must do is get a strong outfit together and go after them. But this time we won't run around blind. We'll figure things out and just keep going until we find them. Then we'll kill the whole bunch of them, even the girl if she gets in our way. After that we'll come back and take up where we left off. If we don't do this to my complete satisfaction, I'm quitting here. There'd be no use in staying."

Traversi licked his dry lips. "I just been out. I'm beat."

"No matter. A good night's rest, then a morning of arranging things, getting a chuck wagon fitted out, fresh horses and the rest of it. We'll go down into that south country on the best-planned manhunt this state ever saw, Red. Any argument on that?"

Red Traversi thought about it for a long time. He could see that dead country again. He could feel the heat, the sting of the grit and the choke of the dust in his lungs. He had the cattle. Edey getting killed didn't worry him any longer. And he admitted to himself he had begun to get sick of Marie with her constant whining about things.

He said, "Why don't you do it on your own, Judge? Then I could stay here and look after things."

Judge Joe Alroe Eggert shook his head and smiled thinly. "I couldn't trust you, Red, you know that. I might be gone a long time and there's the money we put by—I'd be worried all the time that you might light out and I'd never see you again."

Traversi opened his mouth to counter this accusation, but Eggert threw up a hand. "No, Red, it'll be my way. We'll get Cherry and Durant and we'll be showing people that nobody can ride into our territory and cause us trouble."

Eggert moved back to the door as Reg Weedon came in mopping at his sweating brow. "By hell, it's hot, eh?" he commented. When no one answered him, he said, "Heard you missed 'em, Red. Too bad, eh?"

Traversi let out a growl. But Joe Eggert spoke up. "Weedon, Red and I are gonna put you into a position of trust. We want you to take over the management of town for a short time. Sleep in this jailhouse. When we come back, we want everything to be just as we left it—no trouble, no strangers standing tall, nothing different. You understand me, Weedon?"

Weedon gulped. "Where … where are you going?" he stammered out.

"On a trip. Red will explain to you. In the morning, I want you to round up all the boys. We'll have to divide them up and leave some to stay behind with you. Goodnight."

Judge Eggert walked out. He heard Red Traversi swear and it brought a smile to his fat lips. Now, walking slowly down the boardwalk on his way back to the saloon, he thought about his son, Rick. Outcast County had never meant anything to Eggert. Nor did Red Traversi. He decided he didn't even like the man, but he was shackled with him. He shrugged off his thoughts and turned into the saloon.

As Reg Weedon had mentioned, it was indeed a hot night. A good night for drinking.

EIGHT

DEAD OF NIGHT

"Just a minute, Cherry," said Blake Durant as he pulled Sundown off the trail and topped a rise to peer down at the winking lights of Outcast County. The ride across the barren country had produced no worries. Not once had they sighted a rider. They had nursed their horses and taken plenty of rest themselves. Even Ben Adamson looked bright-eyed and fit for fight.

Dane Cherry drew alongside Durant and regarded him coolly. Ever since Durant's warning to him at the campsite the previous evening, he had watched his every move. Cherry was sure that Joyce found the big drifter attractive, but Durant had done nothing to suggest he was interested in her. Cherry was positive he'd have trouble with

Durant, especially when the drifter learned about Cherry's plans for Traversi's money.

"What's wrong now?" Cherry asked as Durant frowned at him.

Durant spoke with authority. "We take only enough money to cover Adamson's cattle, Cherry. Got that?"

Durant's blunt approach sent Cherry back in the saddle. Joyce and Ben Adamson had come up behind them; then, as though sensing something had gone wrong between the two men, Adamson kept his daughter out of earshot. They sat their horses and looked out from the cover of the trees.

"Did I say it would be any different, Durant?" Cherry growled.

"You didn't have to say it, mister—I know what's been on your mind from the minute you changed your mind about coming along. In fact, I've been thinking about going in alone."

Cherry scowled at him. "You trying to play the hero, Durant? Reckon that will make Joyce go beggin' for you?"

A long look passed between them.

"I'm not thinking along those lines, Cherry," Durant finally said. "I offered my help to Adamson because he deserves a few breaks. That's all there is to it."

Cherry was thoughtful. "I could bust the whole mess if you went off alone, Durant. I owe you nothing."

"You wouldn't get it done," Durant warned. "Make up your mind on that here and now. And remember, we take only what we're entitled to."

Cherry's eyes gleamed. "You'd take my word on it, mister?"

"If you give it."

Cherry smiled. "All right, you've got my word. I'll do it your way."

Blake Durant eyed him searchingly.

Cherry went on, "You're a man then who takes chances, Durant. Maybe you gamble some, too?"

"I've gambled in my time. And not only for money."

"Men?"

Blake nodded.

Cherry was grinning broadly now. "How'd you make out last time? Win or lose, drifter?"

"I mostly win. When I lose I learn something."

Dane Cherry straightened in the saddle. Durant always had a way of besting him, in talk or action.

Suddenly Durant said, "Can I trust you, Cherry?"

Cherry pulled at an ear lobe for a moment, then he muttered a curse. "Yes, damn you."

Blake nodded in satisfaction. "Then we'll pull it off, just the two of us. The others will only be in the way."

Cherry turned his horse away as Durant went back to Adamson and Joyce. "Cherry and I are going in alone," Durant said. "We both feel it's better that way. You'd slow us up and Joyce would be a worry."

Ben Adamson frowned back at him. Moonlight cut across his lined face, highlighting the years of worry there ... worry over a ranch, over cattle, over no rain, over a wife dying and a daughter cutting out. Bur his voice was strong and defiant when he said, "This is my business. I won't be pushed aside and treated like a kid. Traversi and his crowd don't worry me one spit."

"If we fail, Ben, somebody will have to look after Joyce. Cherry and I decided that was as important as getting the money for your cattle. So don't argue."

Adamson looked intently at Cherry. "This your idea too, mister?"

"It is," Cherry lied convincingly.

Adamson looked surprised and Joyce regarded Cherry with more warmth than she'd shown the whole day.

Durant said, "We'll go down through the timber and come up behind the town. If things go right we should reach the jailhouse in fifteen minutes and get the safe open in maybe another ten. If things go wrong and we're stopped, we'll fight our way out. Watch for us and be ready to ride."

Adamson still looked put out. But Joyce readily accepted the position. She moved her horse across to Durant and looked into his eyes.

"Be careful," she said.

"I'll be that," he told her.

Cherry straightened in the saddle, plainly disturbed. But Joyce crossed to him and smiled. "You too, Dane. Pa and I will never be able to repay you for what you're doing tonight. Just don't take any unnecessary chances with those hellions. Forget about the money if it's too difficult."

She stood in the stirrups and kissed him on the cheek. Cherry reached for her but Joyce drew back and rejoined her father. By then Durant was already riding into the darkness off the slope, taking a trail across a depression. Cherry put his horse into a run.

"Which one is it, Joyce?" Adamson asked as the sound of hoof beats died in the night's silence.

Joyce looked at him, took a deep breath, and shook her head.

"If it was me, I wouldn't go past Durant, girl. He's all man and made to last. Whatever he does, he'll do it right."

"Dane has helped me a great deal too, Pa," Joyce argued.

"For what he can get out of you, girl. Maybe underneath he has some affection for you and maybe he has enough ability to be a good provider. But I got the feeling that wherever he goes, Dane Cherry will rake up trouble. You could spend a lifetime on the run with him."

Joyce was silent for a long time. She knew she had no right to be thinking of Durant and herself at all. He had never been anything but polite. Yet her father thought she had a chance with him. She wondered about this and then she thought about the woman Durant had lost. How long would the memory of that woman ride with him? How long would his love for her keep him from caring deeply about someone else?

She drew herself straight. "Pa, I'm not like some other women. I don't think that every man who happens along wants me. I know I'm pretty but I don't think it goes deeper than that. Perhaps neither of them will want me permanently."

Adamson waved this down. "They want you, girl. One thing I know about is men. You'll have to choose between them and you'll have to do it quick, before it grows into trouble you won't be able to handle. No sense letting any man, Cherry or Durant, dangle on a string. Each would resent it."

Joyce colored and came out of the saddle. As she walked through the trees, leading her horse, she wondered why life had to be so complex.

Time would tell. Perhaps, when they came back, she would know. If they came back. Her eyes clouded with worry and she settled down to wait, watching her father pace up and down. She knew how disturbed he was. He was a man and he wanted to do a man's work.

"Hold it."

Dane Cherry put a hand on Durant's wrist. The gesture was unnecessary because Durant had already seen the group of men outside the saloon. Red Traversi stood taller than the others, hatless, his thick hair tousled.

Traversi said, "Turn in and get some rest. First light in the morning, Day and Peters will bring the buckboard out here. We'll pack it with plenty of supplies. You others be on hand because we'll be riding out and going fast. Anybody who don't turn up won't need a saddle or a horse again."

Cherry touched Durant's shoulder and pointed back down the laneway. Durant followed him along the lane and across the saloon yard. In the corner of the yard Cherry stepped over a low fence and led the way across a store yard. They reached the jailhouse laneway unchallenged.

Standing in the darkness, gun in hand, Cherry said, "With Edey gone I don't know who Traversi put on to look after the jailhouse. But it'll be somebody Traversi can trust."

Blake Durant said nothing.

"As for blowing that safe," Cherry said, "it might not be necessary. If it's an old model, which is likely in this part of the territory, I might be able to work out the lock combination."

"You've done that before?" Durant asked.

Cherry grinned. "I've been about some, Durant. I had to do lots of things, some legal, some not."

"Just don't go shooting unless it's absolutely necessary," Durant said.

Dane Cherry shrugged, then he moved across the laneway and turned into the jailhouse back yard. His mind warmed at the thought of Traversi's money getting into his pocket. But he'd given Durant his word. Well, if something happened to Durant, his pledge wouldn't count.

Cherry slipped across the yard, stopped at the back steps and pressed his ear to the wall. There was no sound from inside. Cherry stepped up to the door and tried the knob. When it turned in his hand he threw Durant a grin. Blake Durant braced himself, gun in hand. When Cherry eased the door open, he slid into the building beside him. A big man was hunched over the desk reading a tattered magazine. In the cells were Bo Strawbridge and Bede, sitting on opposite bunks. Their heads popped up when they saw the door opening.

Cherry put a finger to his lips and carefully made his way into the room. A board creaked and the big man stirred at the desk, casting a quick look towards the cells. Then Bo Strawbridge called out:

"Bannon, how about a drink?"

"Shut down, Strawbridge!" came the gruff reply, and under cover of the talk Dane Cherry continued towards the desk.

"Hell, I got a thirst a rattler would give away, Bannon. I always treated you fair, didn't I, when I had a stake? Why the hell don't you …"

Bannon had lowered his head again, plainly disinterested in further talk. Then Dane Cherry's gun came down hard. Bannon gave a grunt and slumped forward over the desk.

Bo Strawbridge grinned and called out, "That was neat, Cherry. Now get me them keys. Me and Bede are gettin' to hell out of this town while the goin's good. We want no part of this damn bunch of no-good, boot-lickin' yeller jaspers. They're hardly fit to drink with a man, let alone talk to him. Let us out, eh?"

"Shut down," Cherry told him and crossed to the last cell. He found it locked, then he went back to the office and took the keys from the top drawer of the desk. While he fumbled for the right key, he said, "No need to stand there looking stupid, Durant. Watch the street. If anybody comes, give me due warning."

Blake Durant walked to the window and Bo said, "Get this damn cell open, will you? Traversi has it in for us, Durant. He figures we're tied in with you because we jumped jail when you did. Hell, if it comes to a fight, we might even join in."

"I said to shut down, Strawbridge," said Cherry who was now working at the last cell's lock. He breathed a sigh of relief when he got it open. Walking in, he crossed to a small safe in the corner and knelt down to inspect it.

Bo Strawbridge, watching Cherry anxiously all the time, said, "Traversi opened that tonight, Cherry. I seen him plain. He turned the middle piece right round one way and brought it right back to the top, stopped it there, then went the other way. Damn me, but it came open real easy. How about you deal us in for a slice, eh? Y'see, Traversi cleaned us out before he put us in here. We ain't got a dollar between us and we got thirsts that need maybe fifty dollars to take care of."

Cherry paid him no heed. But he did follow Bo's advice and worked the dial almost as far right as it could go. He pressed his ear hard against the metal until he heard a faint click. Then, grinning, he brought the dial back until he heard a second click. He pulled on the big handle and the safe door opened.

"See, Cherry, didn't I tell you?" Bo Strawbridge cried out. "Now you got to deal us in. Open this cell and we'll take our cut and get to hell outa here. If there's trouble, by hell, you know Bede and me, we ain't no strangers to it."

Cherry still ignored him. Bo cursed. Durant came back to tell him to quieten down. Then Bo started to howl protests and Durant said firmly, "Wait!"

He joined Cherry in the cell. Cherry picked out five bundles of notes and riffled them. Sweat showed on his brow and his eyes gleamed with hunger.

Durant said, "Five thousand is the amount put on the cattle by Adamson. Take only that much."

Cherry gritted his teeth and sucked in his breath. "It's hellion's money," he said.

"No matter. Do as I say."

Durant's gun was pointed at Cherry. The gambler counted and stuffed the money inside his shirt. When he stood up, he stared at the thick bundles of bills stacked on the shelves.

Durant kicked the safe door closed and Bo gave a little cry. "Durant, are you loco? There's a fortune in that safe. By hell, if you don't want it, let me at it. Some of it belongs to Bo and me anyway."

Blake Durant took the keys from Cherry and opened the other cells. Then, as Bo lunged at him, Durant kicked the bottom cell door shut and hurled the keys into the jailhouse yard.

Strawbridge wheeled on Durant, fists lifting, face scarlet with anger. His brother left his cell and regarded Durant curiously. Like his brother he was gunless, but unlike Bo he had no desire to mix it with Durant. In fact, during his stay in the cell, Bede had decided that he'd had enough of brawling with anybody. His head was split open where Traversi's gun butt had struck him and his face was tight from the bruises and gashes received in his saloon yard fight with Bo. Bede told himself that his fighting days were over—after he'd evened the score with Traversi.

"Quit it, Bo," Bede said. "Durant knows what he's doing."

Cherry was standing in the open back doorway. He licked at his lips, craving for the money still running through him.

"Quit?" Bo barked at his brother. "Are you loco, too? Traversi's been drainin' this town dry for months. He's got enough money in there to get us a place of our own."

"We'd never work it," Bede said, then he moved across to the desk, tipped Bannon out of the seat and lifted two gunbelts from a wall hook. He and Bo were buckling their guns on when the front door opened.

Alec Day came a step into the jailhouse, looking bored until he saw the four men. The shock at finding Cherry and Durant there made him reel back. Then his hand went to his gun.

Cherry wheeled, going into a crouch. Before Day's Colt was clear, Cherry's gun exploded.

Day was punched through the doorway by the bullet. He fell to the boards outside, squirmed for a moment and then lay still.

Bo Strawbridge called out, "Come on, Bede, let's get to hell outa here!"

Bede needed no second invitation. Breaking into a run he thundered across the room. Durant looked sourly at Cherry and said:

"Well, that puts out the signals. No matter what happens, stick close to me."

Cherry gave him a disdainful look and went down the steps. The Strawbridge brothers, moving at good speed for such big men, brushed past Cherry, knocking him aside. Bo's boot caught on the ring of cell keys and kicked them further into the yard. Cherry swore.

Then Blake Durant came out, closing the jail-house door behind him. Darkness flooded the yard. Cherry swung his gun around to Durant.

"Damn you!" Cherry clipped out. "All that money …"

Durant said, "We've got a town of hellions to fight, Cherry. Keep your mind on that."

Cherry stood tall, his face working. Then the sound of running steps came from the street boardwalk. Cherry turned and broke into a sprint, heading for the store yard. As he climbed the broken fence, men came streaming from the stables beyond the jailhouse lane. He and Durant were trapped in a crossfire.

Bullets began to whine around them. They ran to the saloon yard where another group of men, led by Judge Joe Alroe Eggert, confronted them. Eggert stepped away from the others, his face black with hate.

"I've been waitin' for you pair!" he snarled and his gun erupted.

Cherry dived to the right, Durant to the left. Then, seeing Cherry getting near the saloon's back door, Durant took his chances and tore across the open yard after him. A bullet tugged at his range coat sleeve and another ripped through his flying bandanna. Durant's hand smashed hard down on

Cherry's back and pitched him forward as a bullet gouged Durant's shoulder. He staggered under the impact of the slug, then he was inside the saloon. As he closed the door he saw a wild-eyed Cherry facing him, gun lifted.

Blake said, coolly, "Get a table up here. I'll watch the front."

Cherry looked undecided for a moment, but when bullets began hammering on the heavy timber of the saloon's door, he turned and dragged a card table to the door. He braced it under the knob and went back for another table, dodging about as bullets howled through the window. Cherry struggled to lift the heavy table onto the other. Then he backed off, firing through the smashed window into the yard.

In the front of the saloon, Durant sent bullets into the main street. Cherry joined him and refilled his gun.

"About ten out here, Traversi among them," Durant said.

Cherry pushed back his hair. Bullets were thudding all along the front wall. Some came through the windows to pound into the inside walls and explode bottles on the bar shelves. Blake Durant, now that he understood the extent of the fight that lay ahead of them, walked coolly around the room and put out the lights. He stood in the gloom and regarded Cherry's dark figure thoughtfully.

If it was to be a fight to the death, he was glad he had a man like Cherry along. He said, "No matter what happens, Cherry, thanks for keeping your word to me. I know how hard it was."

"It was damn near impossible, Durant, and maybe I'd have broken my word given another chance later."

"I know," Durant told him. "So don't try to run out on me if we get a break from here. That money goes to the old man and the girl, no-place else."

Cherry patted the money bulges in his shirt and wondered how long it would be before he ever got his hands on big money like this again. Probably never. He wiped a sleeve over his sweat-gleaming brow and went behind the counter for a bottle of whiskey. He uncorked it and had a long drink; then, after studying Durant for a moment, he handed the bottle across. A barrage of bullets made them both hit the floor. Durant took the bottle and muttered, "Thanks."

"No charge," said Cherry.

NINE

BAD MEN, BAD BUSINESS

Joyce Adamson got up from the ground and swept her long hair back. Her father, despite his determination to be on hand in case of trouble, had been dozing, his body weary from a month of riding.

"Pa, I think they're coming."

Adamson knuckled at his eyes. "You sure, girl?"

"Two riders, Pa. Who else could it be?"

Adamson rose and worked the cramp out of his shoulders. Then he joined Joyce and looked in the direction of her gaze. Sure enough, two riders were coming at a fast clip. Adamson stepped out of the cover of the trees to greet them. But as they slowed at the sight of him, he recognized them as the brothers who'd beaten each other to pulp in the saloon on his first night in Outcast County.

Adamson's hand went to his gun but before he could clear it of the holster, the Strawbridge brothers drew up and Bo's gun covered him.

"What's this?" Bo said in puzzlement as he took stock of Joyce.

"Sure beats me," Bede said, rubbing the back of his neck, looking as perplexed.

Ben Adamson said gruffly, "We were expecting somebody else."

Then Joyce stepped into the moonlight. Bede drew upright in the saddle and pointed at her.

"Damn me, Bo, it's Cherry's woman!"

Bo nodded, having already recognized her. Every time he'd seen Joyce Adamson in town he'd eyed her lustfully. She was about the best looking woman he'd ever laid eyes on, but he'd always known that he couldn't do anything about it except dream. He removed his hat in token of his respect for her.

"And you'd be her father, eh?" Bo asked.

Adamson nodded. "You just come from town?"

"Sure did, and in one hell of hurry. All hell's breaking out in there tonight. If we were a half mile closer, you'd hear it for sure."

Joyce couldn't hide her anxiety. "Did you see Mr. Durant and Mr. Cherry?"

"Yep, ma'am, seen 'em as clear as day. Was them who got us out of the jailhouse. Reckon the whole four of us would have got clean away if it hadn't been for Alec Day showin' up and gettin' himself killed. Bede and me, we're right grateful to them pair of fools for lettin' us get to our horses."

Joyce turned to her father, tears in her eyes. Adamson, after another look at Bo and Bede, nodded grimly. "Thank you for your information. Thank you very much." He turned back towards his horse and Bo and Bede exchanged a worried look.

Bo asked, "What you doin', Mr. Adamson? You ain't thinkin' of goin' in there after 'em, are you?"

"I have to," Ben said. "They went to get money for my stolen cattle. I can't just let 'em die for me; I've got to do what I can."

"They're holed up, Adamson," Bo said. "They must be in the saloon, I reckon, judgin' from the racket comin' from that stinkhole. You won't get one step into town without somebody recognizing you. Then he'll shoot your fool guts out. Better get on that horse and head to hell away from here. We'll ride part of the way if you like, keep you company."

"No," Adamson was adamant despite Joyce's imploring look at him.

The girl's tears made Bede frown. He studied Bo for a moment and said, "It wasn't for them, we'd still be up to our ears in big trouble."

Bo Strawbridge sat back in the saddle, cocking an ear at his brother. "How's that, Bede?"

"We'd still be in that jailhouse, waitin' for Traversi to tear both of us apart. His plan to quit town would'a made him sure we was cut down bad. So I figure that Durant and Cherry saved our hides. Now ... should we leave them to fight on their own or not? I mean, there are two friendly gents up against an outfit that we can't stand the stink of."

Ben Adamson looked curiously at both of them, a spark of hope showing in his eyes. "Do you mean you'll go back?"

Bo pursed his lips and gingerly fingered his swollen lips. He dragged in a ragged breath and finally nodded. "Bede, you're right. We been beltin' each other for so long now that I kinda forgot what it was like to help other folks. But damn me—if you'll excuse me ma'am," he added, looking Joyce's way, "Bede and me were kinda reared on fights. We don't like backin' outa one."

"Then you'll return?" she asked.

"Only on the condition that you and your pa stay out here, ma'am. I reckon that Durant saw how right that was or you wouldn't be here waitin' for him. So, we'll just turn about and see if we can't link up with them."

Joyce beamed at him as she crossed to his horse. "I think you're just wonderful."

Bo blushed and then Joyce reached up and pulled at his shirt. When Bo's face was close enough she kissed him firmly. He bucked back, saying:

"Whoa now, ma'am! That ain't the kind of thing that puts a man in the right frame of mind to kick up hell. You just lay offa me, eh?"

Joyce smiled at him. Bede tipped his hat to Adamson and said, "See you soon. Them friendly jaspers back there have got your money, so I guess we'd best see that it gets to you. Fools they were, only takin' five thousand, but then Durant thinks that way, don't he?"

Bede swung his horse around and Bo hit his mount into a gallop. Together they thundered back towards town.

The Strawbridge brothers entered the gloomy depths of the saloon laneway and listened to the steady thunder of gunshots. Bede looked inquiringly at Bo.

"What the hell are we gonna do now?"

"We'll try the front street," Bo said and pulled out his gun. Moments later Bo saw a group of men on the boardwalk opposite the saloon. He drew back into the shadows, pulling Bede with him.

Then, brightening suddenly, Bo said, "The rooftop. We'll go through Ma Willoughby's place, climb to Carson's roof and get across to the saloon. We'll drop onto the verandah and see if we can get in without being heard. Only we got to watch that Cherry. He's likely to be edgy."

Bede offered no argument. They climbed up a store wall and clambered onto the roof. Removing their boots they made their way across the line of roofs. When they saw the saloon roof before them, Bo told Bede to keep him covered. He leaped out, caught at the verandah post and swung down onto the boards. But his boot caught on the railing top and he pitched forward on his face. When Bede swung in under the verandah a moment later they collided and went sprawling heavily.

Bo pushed Bede away from him. Bede was beginning to resent the rough treatment when two men charged along the verandah. Immediately the brothers forgot their argument and rushed forward. Bo's roundhouse right connected with a man's jaw and sent him crashing through the rail. A piercing scream broke the night's silence and ended with a dull thud. Bede picked up the second

139

man and hurled him at the wall. The man slumped down and did not move.

"A fair start," Bo said. "Now all we got to do is meet up with them friendly jaspers before they gun us down. They were fools leavin' this top section unwatched."

Bede's gaze swept over the verandah. From below came shouts. Together the brothers entered the corridor which separated the guest rooms. Nobody appeared to challenge them. At the top of the stairway, Bo crouched and looked anxiously down. When a bullet howled past his head he called out urgently:

"Hold it, damn you! It's me and Bede!"

"Move and you're dead, mister!" Cherry clipped out.

"Ain't about to move, Cherry," Bo said. "Not till you get it in your head that we're here to help."

There was a moment's silence before Dane Cherry showed himself. He studied the big man intently for some time before he said, "Why, mister?"

"That'd be hard to explain," Bo said. "Can we come down?"

"All right."

Bo moved down the steps. Bede followed, holding his gun firmly, his eyes searching. Before they reached the bottom of the steps, shooting broke out again.

Bo and Bede Strawbridge broke into a run. Durant was crouched at the locked batwings, sending bullets into the street. Outside a man howled in pain. Then Cherry barked:

"If you two are after the money, forget about it."

Bo, his face pressed to the floorboards, looked up angrily. "Now, see here, Cherry, I ain't ever had much time for you, the way you got Bede and me to belt each other around. So don't go makin' out we're thieves. We figured we're obligated to you and anyhow we don't care a spit for the scum followers of Traversi and Eggert. So we met up with the girl and her pa and we decided they'd had enough worry. Anyways, we owe Traversi somethin' for crackin' open Bede's head and beltin' me about some."

Blake Durant studied them. "With your help we might make it. But we'll have to take risks."

Bo chuckled. "Risks, drifter, is what we mostly play with, Bede and me."

Bullets whined through the air about them, smashing more bottles and hammering at the walls. "How many are there, Durant?" Bede asked.

"Ten out front, more out back."

Bo said, "Out back, there's maybe half a dozen, with the judge leading 'em. I seen Traversi out front. If we get them two, the others won't fight much."

Bo stood and looked about him carefully. When he sighted a row of unbroken bottles on a shelf behind the bar, his eyes gleamed and he hurried towards the bar. But another barrage of bullets made him drop to the floor in mid-room. Bede heard a groan come from him and he ran across to Bo who had blood spurting from a hole in his forearm. Bede jerked him up to a sitting position and made him remain still while he pulled a dirty bandanna from his neck and tied it firmly in place over the wound.

Bo growled, "Best get me some whiskey, brother. I sure need it now."

Bede went to the back of the bar and pulled a bottle from the shelf. As he was turning to come back, heavier gunfire from a dozen guns ripped into the saloon. Every bottle on the shelf was shattered and glass rained down on him, soaking his clothes with whiskey before he ducked low and came back to his brother. Bo snatched the bottle from him and drank greedily and Bede had to wrench the bottle away before he could treat himself to a drink.

Meanwhile Cherry and Durant crouched near the batwings taking stock of the activity in the street. Suddenly Cherry let out a string of curses and added, "This stinkin' town!"

Durant shrugged. "Maybe it could be a good town ... for all of us."

Cherry studied him grimly. "You figure to hang on here, maybe settle, get yourself a place and take up with Joyce."

Their looks held for a long moment. Then Blake Durant said, "There's more at stake here than us, Cherry. Can't you see that?"

"No, damned if I can. Traversi's an animal. He means to kill and go on killing till he gets control of this town again. And Joe Eggert is about the foulest, meanest jasper you ever came up against, Durant. I'm cutting out right now."

Blake Durant looked fiercely at him and said, "I'm still holding you to your word. Break it and if we both live through this, I'll find you."

Cherry sat back on his haunches and checked his gun. He said, "I'm moving out now. Do you want to make a break together, or do you figure it more important for me to get away so Adamson can get his money?"

Bo and Bede Strawbridge came across the room slowly, Bo cursing freely and pouring whiskey onto his brother's wound. They eyed Cherry sourly before Bo growled, "We're trapped in this, Cherry, so the only thing to do is to burst out together. Maybe all of us won't make it, but if we stay here and it gets daylight, we're all through. They'll rush us and cut us down."

Cherry nodded. "I've already figured that, Bo. How do you want it? Straight out through that door and each man makes the best he can of it?"

Bo's mouth tightened. He checked with Bede who gave a nod of agreement.

"I'll get the bars down," Bo said.

As Bo walked towards the swing doors, Blake Durant saw him for the real man he was, a fighter who could be stupidly reckless but a man with guts.

Durant said, "Drop the bars and then wait. We'll all go through together. You two head for the jailhouse. Cherry and I will go the other way."

Bo nodded. He knelt at the batwings and slowly withdrew the bars which held the door against them. Stepping back, he felt Bede's heavy breath on the back of his neck. He looked at his brother, gave him a wink and muttered, "Be a breeze, Bede, eh?"

Bede nodded grimly. Durant eased Cherry to his right and positioned himself directly between the batwings. "Open it, Bo," he said.

The gunfire outside had died down. Then, before Durant could move or Bo Strawbridge could open the big doors, Traversi's voice boomed through the silence:

"Durant, I'll make a deal. I just checked my safe. You stole near five thousand dollars from me and the judge. So you throw the money out and we'll give you back your horses. If you don't, that big black is going to get a bullet from me, right between the eyes."

Bo Strawbridge saw anger work in Durant's face. But Durant was in full control of himself. He said, "Open them, Bo. I'll go first. Traversi is directly opposite. He's mine."

Bo lifted a hand and began to pull the doors open. Blake Durant braced himself, then broke into a run. Bo Strawbridge pulled the doors wide open and Durant burst through. He surprised two men crouched behind the saloon trough. When they rose, guns lifting, Durant sent two fast shots at them. One spun around and fell and the other ran from the trough into the darkness across the street. Wild gunfire erupted.

Then Dane Cherry was coming through the batwings and pounding down the boardwalk. The Strawbridge brothers came out together and broke into wild flight towards the jailhouse end of the town. As they went, hellions converged on them from the opposite boardwalk. Bo cursed and let Bede run on as he saw that Durant was held down by heavy gunfire coming from all sides. Labeling himself a fool, Bo doubled back to help Durant and saw Dane Cherry running for the deep darkness at the far end of the street.

Bo called, "Damn you, Cherry, you blasted coward!"

Bo drew up beside Durant and snapped, "Let's get to hell outa here. We ain't got no chance in the open."

Blake gave him a grateful look and pointed down the opposite boardwalk with his gun.

"Traversi's there," he said. "Cover me."

Blake Durant went forward, firing at both sides of the store before him. A bullet tugged at his coat and another burned a line down his neck. He felt blood soaking into his shirt where his previous wound had opened. To hell with it. Then he saw Red Traversi, the tin star on his shirt betraying his presence in a store doorway. Bo Strawbridge's gunfire had sent three other hellions backing off and when Bede joined his brother, cursing him for a fool, Blake Durant knew that his initial opinion of these wild living jaspers had been right on line.

But Dane Cherry had run. And Cherry had the Adamson money. Blake Durant was sour about that but for the moment his war was with Red Traversi. He put two more gun hands to flight and dropped to the dust just short of the storefront boardwalk. Traversi had held his fire until this moment; now, realizing that Durant had caught him out, he showed himself and his big gun was barking. He came two strides out of the doorway, face distorted with hate.

"Damn you, Durant, damn you to hell!"

Blake Durant's first bullet knocked Traversi back a pace, and his second tore his chest open. Traversi went staggering to the wall, then pushed himself off. His gun belched flame and Durant felt the burn of a bullet along his right side. Traversi had guts, more than Durant had given him credit for.

"Drop your gun and it's over," Blake called out to him.

Traversi grunted an oath at him and shot again. Behind Durant, Bo Strawbridge said, "Don't give him no quarter. He ain't like other folks. He's lived a lie too damned long."

Blake saw Traversi's lips peel back in a snarl of rage. His face went dark, his eyes disappearing in his dark eye sockets. Then he took a hesitant step forward, reached for the wall to support himself but didn't make contact with it. He fell onto his side. But he wasn't dead. He lifted his gun and Durant put another bullet into his chest. Traversi dropped the gun and slumped back against the wall, blood pouring from his wounds. He opened his mouth to speak but only a spurt of blood came from his lips. Then he pitched forward, onto his face.

Bo Strawbridge and his brother Bede joined Durant. They stood covering each other as the hellions backed off. But, before they could begin to congratulate themselves, Blake Durant sighted Dane Cherry at the street's end. A barn stood there, tall in the gloom of the street. Near the doorway were three men and two tethered horses; one horse was Sundown.

Durant said, "Bo, Bede, you've done enough. Head out while the going's good."

Durant went on then, disregarding the gun hands still backing away. He was within a hundred yards of Dane Cherry when he saw spurts of gunfire come from the barn doorway. Sundown reared high, lashing out with his hoofs.

Then Judge Joe Eggert, bleeding from a gash in his right cheek and walking with a limp, came down the far boardwalk. Cherry and Eggert clearly saw each other at the same time.

For a brief moment there was indecision between them, then Joe Eggert proved what Blake Durant already knew. Although weakened by gun wounds and slowed by his limp, he came off the boardwalk with his big gun bucking in his hand. He showed contempt for Cherry's efforts to cut him down. Then, although he staggered from the impact of another bullet, Joe Eggert, gunfighter and self-appointed judge, triggered four bullets that tore Cherry's body apart. As Dane Cherry fell limply to the dust, his shirt came open and five thousand dollars spilled out.

Blake Durant halted in mid-street. Bo and Bede Strawbridge, both slightly wounded, came up from behind and stood on either side of Durant.

Durant called, "Eggert, drop it!"

Joe Alroe Eggert wheeled about, his gun still smoking from the shots he had put into Dane Cherry. His face was clouded with hate for Blake Durant.

Durant said, "It's all over. You'll collect rope, Eggert, for the murder of innocent men."

Eggert sneered at him, then his gun swung up. Bo Strawbridge, thinking Durant a fool to have waited this long, threw himself to the side and Bede went the other way. But Blake Durant stood his ground, his gun held steady.

Joe Alroe Eggert faced Durant on wide-planted feet. His shirt was open down the front showing thick gray hair matted with blood. Loathing for Durant twisted his features. Across the street townsmen were forming in silent groups and not a man showed any intention of coming closer. Eggert shifted back into the barn shadows and his gun barked.

Blake Durant still held his fire, aware that Sundown was rearing behind Eggert. The horse kicked up a tremendous amount of dust which began to make a screen of cover for Eggert.

Then Bo Strawbridge called out, "Hell, Durant, watch it! Get him now!"

Eggert's gun still blasted away, but this time his shots were directed in Bo's direction. Yelping from the burn of a bullet Bo rolled over and kicked himself furiously into the cover of Dane Cherry's body. Another bullet slammed into Cherry with a sickening thud. Bede, who had run doubled-over for the barn wall, skidded to a halt when he heard his brother call out. Wheeling he saw Eggert dodge Sundown's thrashing legs. Bede's gun lifted.

Durant called, "Hold it, Bede."

Bede Strawbridge scowled back at him, but held his fire until he saw three figures break away from the barn's wall. Dropping into a crouch he hammered off shots.

"Damn you, Bede," Durant yelled angrily at him and hurried forward. But he had gone only three paces when he saw a man lurch drunkenly into the open clutching at his throat. He was followed by a second, who went down under the hail of bullets from Bo Strawbridge's gun.

Sundown was rearing again, straining back against the tautness of a tie rope attached to the barn's tin wall. A section of the tin buckled and finally tore loose. Sundown lashed out in terror and snorted in fright and Eggert lunged past the big stallion and threw himself into the barn doorway.

As the darkness swallowed the Judge, Bo Strawbridge threw himself out of the way of Sundown as the big horse, dragging the sheet of tin, tore past Cherry's unmoving body. Still rolling, Bo sighted the last of the three gun hands running and shooting back across his shoulder at Bede. Bo's gun bucked and the gun hand went down on his chest, skidded a yard and came to rest in a pool of light thrown onto the dust from the opposite boardwalk.

Blake Durant halted just short of the barn doorway. He had seen Eggert go in, but could hear no sound from inside. He checked on Sundown's wild progress down the town and seeing the horse wheel around the corner of the street, he brought his gaze back to the dark hole before him. Bo Strawbridge, nursing his right elbow, drew alongside him and flattened himself against the wall. Bede joined him, saying,

"Where'd he go, Durant?"

"He's inside."

Bede looked frowningly at him and threw out his hand to halt Bo, as Bo, his taste for fight in no way satisfied, started for the doorway.

Durant put himself in front of both of them and said, "Watch the back. This way's mine."

Not waiting for argument, Blake Durant braced himself and lunged into the doorway. The snarl of a bullet sent him dodging to the side.

Durant called, "You've got no chance, Eggert. Throw down your gun."

His answer come in a blast of wild gunfire from behind the last stall. Durant moved with the ringing echo of the shots deafening him. He went straight at Eggert, his own gun blasting away. The bullets rammed into the far wall and tore through. Eggert had stopped firing. Blake went down on his stomach in the dark and filled his gun. He was still lying flat when Eggert's gunfire started again, first a single shot, placed to Blake's right, then a string of shots to the left. Blake did not move. He lifted his gun and aimed below the last stall. Then he waited. Time stood still and there was no noise at all.

"Durant?"

The call came from the back of the barn up which a cool blast of night wind suddenly came. Blake Durant did not answer.

There was a sudden clamor of movement followed by the thud of bodies on the straw-strewn floor.

"Durant, you all right?"

It was Bo Strawbridge's voice, ringed with concern. Blake wanted to call to him to stay back because he felt he had Eggert's full measure here.

But to make a sound at all would betray his position to Eggert. And Blake Durant, conditioned by many similar situations, had the patience to bide his time, until morning if Eggert insisted.

So he lay there, unmoving, listening while scratching sounds told him that Bo and Bede were crawling towards him. How long Eggert would hold his fire he had no idea but he knew that Eggert's hate for any man who bucked him would not permit him to pass up an opportunity to kill one or both of these reckless cowhands.

It was only a minute later that a tongue of flame burst upwards from darkness below the row of stalls. Within seconds that flame was a fire leaping brightly from out of a hay heap. Furtive shadows fell back from the side of the heap and then Joe Eggert made his last desperate move.

A vicious curse was drowned under the blast of gunfire and then Eggert came limping out of his cover. The fire caught the wild, mad gleam in his eyes as he went past the flaming hay heap towards the section Blake Durant had seen the Strawbridge brothers retreat to. Eggert's gun kept punching out shots as he pounded his way up towards Durant.

Slowly Blake Durant came to his feet. Eggert looked his way but his scowling face was filled with uncertainty. And fear. He quickly prodded bullets into his gun and drawing in a deep breath, broke into a run. Blake Durant moved to block his way and Eggert, finally sighting him, let out a gasp.

Then all the hate that had twisted Eggert's mind into that of a loco killer, tore out of him. The fear left him. The uncertainty fled his features. He came to a halt within a few paces of the barn doorway and the freedom beyond it. A few paces too many, and his face reflected his knowledge of that.

"But for you, Durant," he snarled. "But for you, damn you!"

Eggert's gun exploded but the noise was lost in the thunder of Durant's Colt. Eggert rocked back and his knees gave way. He fell on his face and lay still.

Bo and Bede Strawbridge came slowly out of the smoke-filled barn and stopped close to Eggert's bullet-torn, bloodied body. Neither of them spoke. Their gazes lifted to take in Blake Durant and he said simply, "Time to cut out," and walked towards the barn doorway. He spared a glance for the dead gun hands before he went on. Bo and Bede watched him for some time before Bede nudged his brother and led the way to where the horses were tethered.

Blake Durant walked the middle of the street to where an old-timer stood holding Sundown on a short tie-line. The big horse pulled towards him and Durant put out his hand. The old-timer looped the line over Durant's grimy palm and said,

"He sure made some racket goin' uptown, Durant. So did you, eh?"

Blake said nothing. He swung onto Sundown and turned him back towards Bo and Bede Strawbridge. Drawing rein, Blake Durant watched the fire take stronger hold on the barn. Inside lay a dead Joe Alroe Eggert. Within the hour Eggert's body would be nothing but cinders. He turned Sundown past Bo Strawbridge, meaning to go on, but Bo said,

"What about Traversi's hoard?"

"Leave it for the town."

"For these cowardly fools?"

"It was their money."

Bo shook his head. "They lost it once. Hell, they're born losers."

"The odds against them were too great and they didn't know how to fight before. Maybe they've learned something. Anyway, what you've done tonight proves you're not thieves, Bo. Leave it at that."

Bo wiped a line of sweat from his face and looked at his brother. Bede's right eye had closed where Bo had struck him in their last fight. Suddenly he was sorry that he had hurt his brother.

Then Durant rode to where Dane Cherry lay. The sound of hoof beats came from the far end of town. Looking that way, Durant saw seven riders hit the trail north. He knew that this was the last of the Traversi-Eggert bunch, hired guns who'd seen the end of an era in Outcast County and wanted no part of what would follow.

Durant came out of the saddle, collected the banknotes and stuffed them into his saddlebag. As he swung back into the saddle and made his way down the street, Bo and Bede Strawbridge went to their horses.

Townsmen began to show themselves along both sides of the street. They looked at this loner, Blake Durant, and wondered what manner of man he was. On their faces was a gratitude but Blake Durant wanted no part of it. No one bothered to approach him. They merely watched him ride past.

Bo Strawbridge sat in the cookhouse and eyed his thick steak eagerly. It had been a long ride back to Adamson's ranch. Durant had handed across the money taken from Traversi's safe and spent a long time with Ben Adamson on the porch of the big house. That had been last night and Bede and Bo, on rising, had discussed with Adamson the likelihood of their staying and helping out until they got on their feet again. Ben Adamson had only been too keen to keep them on.

When Durant walked into the cookhouse, Bo grinned up at him. "Guess you'll be staying too, eh, Durant?"

"Why do you figure that, Bo?"

Bo looked surprised at the question. "Hell, the girl. You ain't gonna cut out on her, are you? You ain't that kind of a fool."

Bede entered the cookhouse behind Durant and eyed Bo's steak hungrily. Bo glared warningly at him and pulled his plate a little closer. The smell of the steak made Bo's nostrils twitch.

"I'll be moving on, Bo," Durant said.

Bo gaped and Bede moved behind him, plucking a fork from the stove side bench. He licked his lips and looked across Bo's shoulder at the steak.

"You mean you'd leave a little lady like that out here on her own and ride away? Hell, are you already married or somethin', Durant?"

"No."

"Why then? She's set her hat at you, no mistake. Hell, all you got to do is …"

"Best of luck in the future, Bo. You too, Bede. Been fine knowing you. Maybe one day we'll meet again."

Bo stood up, put out his hand and grinned. "Durant, meetin' you's been fine, real fine."

While Blake Durant took the big man's hand, Bede slipped in beside him and forked the steak out of the plate. He winked at Durant with his unclosed eye and bit a huge chunk out of the steak.

"Bede," said Bo, turning to check his brother. "Say goodbye to …"

Bo's talk stopped there. He saw the steak, saw his brother chewing and his fists lifted. "By hell, Bede, of all the sneakin', thievin', low-bellied jaspers I ever met in my life, you'd be the best."

Bede waved him away. "Bo, we said we wasn't gonna fight each other no more. We said …"

"To hell with what we said," barked Bo, and his big fist caught Bede on the other eye. Bede staggered back under the power of the blow, hit the wall and bounced off it. He glared at his brother, then took another bite of the steak and pitched it back onto the stove.

Bo hurled himself across the table and Bede grabbed him by the back of the shirt and flung him at the wall. Blake Durant moved into the cookhouse doorway and leant against the doorjamb.

Bo came off the wall holding his head in his hand. Blood ran from between his clenched teeth. His eyes were wild with bitterness.

"Why you polecat-bred, stinkin' damn …"

Bede's fist slammed the words back into Bo's mouth and Bede gave a grunt of satisfaction.

"Never learn, Bo, never should you live to be a hundred. All the time you start somethin' you ain't got no chance of finishin'. This time, this last time, you can bet, I'm gonna teach you proper and that'll be the end of it."

Blake Durant turned his back on them and while the two brothers punched themselves stupid for the ownership of a piece of meat, he walked out, smiling.

Blake went to the barn, saddled up Sundown and rode him down the clearing. He stopped short of the big house porch and waited for Ben Adamson to come out. They had spent a lot of time talking the previous night and understood each other perfectly. Blake hoped Adamson had explained things to Joyce afterwards. One day he might come back. He might. He didn't know. A memory still tugged at him, keeping him confused. Until that memory released him, he couldn't find happiness with a fine young woman like Joyce Adamson.

Adamson, seeing the worry in Durant's face, said, "It's all right, Blake. She knows."

Durant looked beyond him to the open doorway of the house. There was no sign of Joyce.

"It's best this way, Blake," Adamson said. "You said that one day you might drop in. Don't make it too far in the future, eh?"

"I'll try not to."

He sent Sundown running and the fully rested horse pounded into the distance, eager, like the man in the saddle, to put this place behind him. Durant eased the horse to a canter and looked back from the rise. Joyce was standing with her father now and even from that distance he could see the hurt in her eyes. He lifted his right arm and they waved back.

The cookhouse door suddenly came splintering out and Bede Strawbridge, reeling, followed it. Bo staggered out after him, fists still pumping. Blake breathed a sigh of relief, touched his golden bandanna and put Sundown into a run again.

Where would it stop? When would it stop? The next town, the next month? He touched at the reins and Sundown thundered down the slope towards the little creek, then Blake Durant returned to the loneliness which was his life.